No way out

"Call," Sharon hissed. Only then did Mack notice the cordless phone clutched in Sharon's left hand.

Sweat began trickling down McKenzie's forehead. A salty drop ran into her eye, but she made no attempt to wipe it away. She swallowed and felt the edge of the knife against her throat. "Call who?"

The knife pressed harder. "Don't be a fool, Mack. Call your parents. Your parents, Mack. Tell them you're going to spend the weekend with me."

Titles in <u>The Power</u> series

by Jesse Harris

THE
POWER

Where
horror
waits...

The Obsession

by Jesse Harris

Borzoi Sprinters · Alfred A. Knopf · New York

Library of Congress Cataloging-in-Publication Data
Harris, Jesse.
The obsession / by Jesse Harris.
p.   cm. — (The Power ; #8)
Summary: McKenzie Gold's friendship with Sharon Roderick, the
new girl in town, turns deadly when Sharon starts to abuse
McKenzie's psychic powers.
ISBN 0-679-83670-5
[1. Extrasensory perception—Fiction.   2. Emotional problems—
Fiction.   3. Interpersonal relations—Fiction.]   I. Title.
II. Series: Harris, Jesse. Power ; #8.
PZ7.H24190b   1992
[Fic]—dc20   92-19506
RL: 4.5
First Borzoi Sprinter edition: February 1993

Manufactured in the United States of America
10 9 8 7 6 5 4 3 2 1

New York, Toronto, London, Sydney, Auckland

chapter 1

"*You know what* I'm in the mood for?" McKenzie Gold asked.

Lilicat answered immediately. "Making out with Mel Gibson."

McKenzie giggled into the phone. She could usually count on Lilicat to say the first thing that came into her head. That was one of the many things she liked about her best friend.

It was a Sunday evening in early December. A freezing wind was whipping through the town of Lakeville, rattling windows and chilling bones. McKenzie sat on the floor of her cozy room, just inside the door; that was as far as the hall phone stretched.

"Actually," McKenzie said, "I was thinking

more like pizza." She ran her hands through her long auburn hair before adding, "And just in case you were right about me owing you that money—which of course you weren't—I'll make it my treat."

Lilicat snorted. "Hang on. Let me check with my mom." The phone clunked down.

McKenzie smiled. She and Lilicat had been friends so long it was almost impossible for them to stay mad at each other. The two girls had argued at the mall just that morning, when McKenzie had asked to borrow ten bucks to buy the new R.E.M. tape and Lilicat had claimed she still owed her for the last one. But now, as Mack waited for Lilicat to get back on the phone, she was sorry she'd made such a big deal about the whole thing.

As if sensing that McKenzie was now on "hold," her old black cat, Blue, trotted over and rubbed his ear hard against her jeans.

"Sorry, Blue," McKenzie said as she gently scratched under his chin. "No pizza for you." She picked up the cat, kissed him on the nose, then set him back down on the floor.

McKenzie walked the phone back out into the hall. "MOM?! DAD?!" she yelled. "DO YOU MIND IF LILICAT AND I GO OUT TO EAT?"

Two doors down, Shelby Gold stuck his head

out of his bedroom. McKenzie's father had a large, round face; she often felt the urge to pinch his cheeks like a baby's. Right now, though, he looked a little annoyed. "What are you yelling about?" he demanded. "I'm not deaf—yet!"

"I'm sorry, I thought you were downstairs," McKenzie said sheepishly. "I just wanted to know if Lilicat and—"

"I heard you, believe me," he said. "What's the matter? You afraid of a little old-fashioned home cooking?"

For the past few Sundays, Mr. Gold had been giving his wife one night off a week in the kitchen. As much as she loved her dad, McKenzie had to admit that cooking was not his greatest talent. Last Sunday, for instance, he had accidentally tripled the amount of pepper in a recipe, which McKenzie's eight-year-old brother Jimmy had promptly dubbed "The Tuna Casserole of Death."

"It's not that," McKenzie said, kindly. "It's just that I'm kind of in the mood for pizza."

Mr. Gold's face fell for an instant, but soon perked up. "Oh, well, at least you're not missing tuna casserole night!" Suddenly Shelby sniffed the air—"Uh-oh"—and hurried down the stairs.

"It's a go," Lilicat said, coming back on the line. "What should we get on the pizza?"

McKenzie could hear her father groaning in

the kitchen as the smell of charred food wafted up the stairs. "Onions," she said.

"*Onions?* You never get onions."

"That's just when Aidan's around. I don't want to get bad breath and gross him out. But since he's puffing on his tuba miles away, I can eat all the onions and garlic I want." The mere thought of her boyfriend, Aidan Collins, brought a lump to McKenzie's throat. He played the tuba in the school band, which had been chosen to participate in a national tour. It was a big deal—the band members were going to be away for two whole weeks. It seemed like forever to McKenzie.

"Okay, onions," agreed Lilicat. "How about some green peppers too? I'll call it in and—" Lilicat was interrupted by a shrill blast of sound. "Hey, what's that noise?" she asked.

"The smoke alarm," said McKenzie, covering her ears.

"Oh, I almost forgot," Lilicat said. "It's Sunday night. Your dad's in the kitchen, right?"

"You guessed it," McKenzie said, laughing. "I'll pick you up in five minutes."

When McKenzie walked into the kitchen a minute later, her father was bent over the trash can, trying to scrape black crust off a roasting pan, and her mom was opening the windows to let the smoke out.

"It's all right, Joanne," Mr. Gold said. "You can go back to your book. Everything's under control. And I think a lot of this meat loaf can be saved."

"Shelby," Joanne Gold began, her blue eyes twinkling. "If you'd like me to—"

"Not at all, dear," Shelby said quickly. "I said I was cooking, and that's just what I'm going to do."

McKenzie and her mom exchanged amused glances. "You want the car keys, right?" Mrs. Gold asked. She fished in her purse and handed over the key chain, whispering, "Smart move."

"I heard that," called Shelby.

Jimmy entered from the den wearing an L.A. Raiders T-shirt that extended below his knees. "The Raiders just got totally wiped," he announced. "Schroeder threw four intercep—" He stopped in mid-sentence. "Fire . . . everyone out of the house, quick!"

Mr. Gold raised a rubber spatula in warning. "You better watch it, Jimmy, or . . . or . . . or you're not getting any," he finished lamely.

Mrs. Gold and her two children burst out laughing. After a moment, Mr. Gold joined in as well.

The night sky was perfectly clear; the cold winter wind stung McKenzie's cheeks. As she backed her mom's Volvo out of the driveway, someone flicked on the Golds' porch light so it would be on when she returned.

McKenzie smiled as she turned onto the road. She had just gotten her license that year—the minute she'd turned sixteen. But Mack had already made this short trip so many times, she felt as if the car knew the way to Lilicat's by itself, like a horse trotting back to the barn.

McKenzie and Lilicat went way back. They had met as five-year-olds in Miss Winemuller's kindergarten class. Five years old, McKenzie mused. That was only one year after the nightmares had begun.

McKenzie shuddered at the memory.

Night after night she had awakened screaming—long, bloodcurdling screams coming from an otherwise happy, normal four-year-old girl. McKenzie's worried parents had taken her to a psychologist, who assured them the nightmares would pass.

The psychologist was right: The nightmares had finally subsided. But then, in the last few years, it had all started again—the nightmares, as well as strange visions that came to her when she was awake. Once she had terrible visions of a man who murdered baby-sitters. As it turned out, these murders really were happening, and she'd managed to piece together enough clues from her visions to help the police catch the killer. Another time her visions had actually saved Aidan's life. McKenzie had learned to take these visions very seriously. They always contained important messages of some kind, about the past, the present, or the future.

Besides Aidan, Lilicat was the only friend McKenzie had ever trusted with this secret. McKenzie felt that if people knew she had special abilities, they would treat her like a freak, and she'd have no chance for a normal life. But Mack knew she could trust Lilicat completely. She'd never betray her secret.

The porch light was on at the Caine house as well, and when McKenzie pulled into the driveway, the curtain in Lilicat's second-story bedroom fell back into place. A moment later, the front door opened and a sixteen-year-old girl with dark, flowing hair came bouncing out onto the porch.

"I forgive you," Lilicat said as she got into the car.

"For what?" teased McKenzie. "For yelling at me?"

"For everything," Lilicat said with a grin. She studied her face in the rearview mirror, applying a layer of red lip gloss to her pouty lips. "Did I tell you what Alec called me yesterday?"

"Yes," McKenzie said, pulling out.

Lilicat giggled. "Okay, but can I tell you again?" She didn't wait for permission. "He said I was the most exotic girl he's ever seen. Isn't that funny? I don't think I'm exotic—do you?" She jutted her face toward the mirror, searching for signs of exoticism.

"You're great-looking and you know it," McKenzie said. "I'd love to have your looks."

"Give me a break, Mack. If you looked like me you wouldn't have those long legs—or that hair!" She had always admired McKenzie's long, thick, auburn hair.

For once, the parking lot outside Pizza Town wasn't crowded with bikes and cars. In fact, the only other car was a shiny red Audi with a vanity license plate that read FOREVER.

The two girls dashed through the windy lot and into the warm pizza parlor.

"Oh, how cute!" exclaimed Lilicat as soon as the door closed behind them. She crouched down. A fluffy little white dog with black eyes was jumping up and down at her feet.

McKenzie stooped to pet the dog. "Look at his eyes," she said. "Little black buttons."

"How did you know her name was Buttons?" said a sultry voice.

McKenzie looked around. There was only one other customer in the restaurant. Standing at the counter was a tall, pretty blond girl wearing an unzipped green parka and cowboy boots. She was smiling at McKenzie and Lilicat. McKenzie smiled back and shrugged. "I didn't," she said.

"I told you to take that dumb dog out of here," said a grouchy-looking man behind the counter.

"Buttons," the girl called. The dog turned and scampered back toward her.

"I said out!" the counterman repeated.

"I know, but you gave me the wrong toppings." The girl gestured at the small pie steaming in its box on the counter. "I ordered pepperoni and *mushrooms*," she explained.

"All right, all right," the counterman said. "Just hold on a second." He turned to Lilicat and McKenzie.

"I ordered a small, with onions and peppers," Lilicat told him.

"It's coming right out." The pizza man slid a wooden board into the oven, pulled out a bubbling pie topped with peppers and mushrooms, and slid it into a cardboard box.

"Uh, that's pepper and mushroom," McKenzie pointed out. "We ordered peppers and onions."

The man threw up his hands. "What are you girls making trouble for me for?"

McKenzie glanced at the blond girl again and caught her staring back. "You go to Lakeville High, don't you?" the girl asked with a small, shy smile.

McKenzie nodded. The girl grinned. "Yeah, I thought so. I'm new. Sharon Roderick."

The girl's soft smile was infectious. McKenzie smiled back. "I'm McKenzie Gold, and this is—"

"Lilith Caine, but you can call me Lilicat."

"And I'm Mike," the man behind the counter muttered sarcastically. "Now do you mind if we get back to the pies?"

"Sorry," said McKenzie. "But it looks like you mixed up our two orders."

"No way," said the counterman. "I took both the orders myself. Here are the receipts."

"So that's what happened," Lilicat said. "You wrote down the orders wrong. We—"

"Hey!" McKenzie suddenly yelped.

"Buttons," said Sharon, looking embarrassed. "Stop it!"

The tiny white dog was busily untying McKenzie's sneaker lace with her teeth.

"That's okay," McKenzie said, laughing. "What kind of dog is it?"

"Maltese. She's only a puppy, and I don't

really have her trained yet." Sharon scooped up the dog and held her in one hand. The dog seemed to be smiling at them. "She's already just about as big as she's going to get, though," added Sharon, grinning fondly at the dog.

"She's adorable," Lilicat gushed.

Sharon smiled proudly. "Do you guys have pets?"

"I have a cat," McKenzie said. "But I don't think he and Buttons would get along. Blue *hates* dogs."

"And vice versa," added Lilicat.

"So what do you want to do here?" said the counterman, glaring at them.

"Well," McKenzie said hesitantly. "The thing is, I really have a craving for onions."

"And I had my heart set on mushrooms," said Sharon.

The counterman threw up his hands. "You want me to make you two new pies? I can make you new pies. But you'll have to wait about fifteen minutes."

The three girls were silent. Then Lilicat said, "I've got an idea. Why don't we all eat together and share both pies? That way, everyone gets what they want."

"Sounds good to me," McKenzie said, and turning to Sharon she asked, "Okay with you?"

"Gee, I don't know," Sharon said. "Since I'm

new here, I kind of had my heart set on not making any new friends."

McKenzie stared at the blond girl for a beat, not quite sure she had heard right. Then she laughed. A sense of humor, too! McKenzie was beginning to like this Sharon. "It's a deal then," she said, grinning.

"The next question," said Lilicat, "is where."

"We can go to my house," Sharon offered. "We've got loads of room. Not a lot of furniture, but plenty of room."

"Great," said McKenzie. This was starting to feel like an adventure. "Do you need to check with your parents first or anything?"

"Nope. My mom will be overjoyed."

"Then that's that," said Lilicat enthusiastically.

A big smile spread across Sharon's face. "I knew it was a good idea to get pizza!" she said.

Lilicat and McKenzie both smiled too. The counterman turned back to his oven.

Sharon led the way in her red Audi. McKenzie and Lilicat followed.

Sharon drove right past Mack's house. McKenzie smiled. The "Gold Residence," as her father referred to it, was a rambling old Victorian two-story house with a rickety wraparound porch. It needed a paint job, but it still looked very friendly, somehow. Mack caught a glimpse of Jimmy jumping around in the living room.

Five more blocks, then Sharon turned onto Oak Lawn.

DEAD END announced the yellow reflective sign.

The red Audi eased down the long street and pulled up in front of a large, ultramodern house with odd angles and tall, narrow windows. Most of the windows were dark. "I didn't know this place had been sold," McKenzie said to Sharon as the three girls piled out of their cars. "My mother's a realtor, and she showed the house to a few clients." Mack didn't add that her mom had predicted it would never be sold. It was off by itself, isolated on an undeveloped street.

"Isn't it a little creepy living all the way at the end of a dead end like this?" asked Lilicat.

McKenzie winced. Count on Lilicat to be brutally direct!

But Sharon didn't seem offended. "Actually, I love it," she said, deadpan. "Way out in the sticks, no neighbors to hang out with . . . it's a teenage girl's dream!"

From Lilicat's expression, Mack could tell her friend wasn't sure how to take this. "She's kidding," McKenzie said helpfully.

"I know," Lilicat giggled as Sharon stepped

ahead and buzzed the doorbell with her elbow. She was holding Buttons in one hand and the pizzas in the other.

When the door swung open, McKenzie's first thought was that Sharon had instantly aged thirty years. The woman who stood before them had Sharon's tall, thin frame, her clear blue eyes, blond hair, and shy smile.

"Mom?" Sharon said eagerly. "Look what I brought home! Can you believe it? Friends!" She laughed an easy laugh and gestured with her full arms. "This is Lilith Caine, and this is McKenzie Gold. Is it all right if they—"

"Of course, sweetie, that's wonderful," her mom broke in, flashing another warm but distracted smile. "Come on in, kids, I'm just—" She had already turned and was heading back into the house.

Mrs. Roderick picked up the phone, which was lying on the side table. "Hold on just one sec," she mouthed to the girls; then, into the phone she said, "Sorry. It's Sharon and some—" She turned back and gave them another wide smile. "Some girlfriends."

The smile faded quickly. "Oh, I just don't know," she sighed, apparently resuming an interrupted conversation. "Now he says he wants the lawyers to handle all that. I know it's not

good for me to see him, but it still"—her voice
caught on the final word—"hurts." She sighed
deeply and, for the sake of privacy, turned quickly
toward the wall.

Sharon rolled her eyes for Mack and Lilicat's
benefit, whispering, "Love trouble. That's all
she talks about since my dad left." She led them
past her mother and into a large, mostly empty
dining room. A large-screen TV was tuned to
the evening news. The dining-room table was
covered with boxes, and there weren't any chairs.
"Like I said," Sharon laughed, "not a lot of
furniture. We haven't finished unpacking. Let's
eat up in my room."

Sharon handed the two pizzas to Lilicat while
the dog yipped at their feet. Then she swung
open the large refrigerator door and pulled out
a two-liter bottle of Diet Slice. She took a carton
of fat-free fudge ripple ice cream from the freezer,
then paper plates, napkins, and plastic silver-
ware from a box on the counter. "We're outta
here," she called over her shoulder, leading the
way up the long front staircase.

Sharon's mom didn't even look up as they
filed past. Talk about distracted, McKenzie
thought.

McKenzie gasped as Sharon opened the door
to her room and flicked on the light.

"Wow," said Lilicat.

"Wow," Mack agreed.

Sharon blushed. "It's not all set up yet, but . . ."

McKenzie's eyes traveled around the room and stopped at an open pink parachute hanging from the ceiling. It made her feel as if she were inside a big tent. Sharon's bed was huge, circular, and covered with throw pillows. The walls were decorated with several framed movie posters, including one of Keanu Reeves. Lilicat walked right over to it.

" 'For Sharon,' " Lilicat read the inscription. " 'With love . . .' " She looked up, shocked. "Mack!" she squealed. "Look at this. It's signed by Keanu himself!"

McKenzie peered over Lilicat's shoulder, impressed.

"My uncle is an assistant producer," Sharon explained. "I didn't meet Keanu or anything; my uncle just got him to sign it for me."

"Just?" Lilicat was impressed.

Sharon pushed the play button on her tape deck and a rock song blared. "R.E.M.'s new album!" Mack exclaimed.

"You like R.E.M.?"

McKenzie poked Lilicat. "Yeah, I would have

bought that tape today but Lilicat wouldn't lend me the money."

"Don't start that again," Lilicat warned. But her tone was light.

"If you give me a blank tape, I can copy it for you," Sharon offered. "I've got a tape-to-tape."

"Great!"

"You see," said Lilicat. "I *saved* you money."

"Thanks a lot," Mack said. "Now how about saving me from this vicious dog?"

Buttons was running around the room, jumping up on each of the girls in turn. Sharon patted the dog's head and let her lick her hand. "That's what I love about Buttons," she said. "It takes so little to make her happy. Don't you wish you could get this excited about coming home?"

Sharon knelt on the floor and opened both pizza boxes. "Help yourself," she told her guests.

McKenzie lifted a slice and took her first chewy, cheesy bite. She closed her eyes and moaned happily. "You know," she said, "I think pizza is the one thing that's always as good as you think it's going to be."

"I think Buttons agrees with you," Lilicat said.

"Buttons!" Sharon shrieked. "Stop it." The

little dog was prancing on her hind legs, dark button eyes begging soulfully.

"I'd better not give her anything," Sharon explained. "The last time she had pepperoni she threw up all over my mother's bed."

McKenzie laughed. "So," she said with her mouth full, "where are you and Buttons from?"

"Cadaret."

"Why did you move?" Lilicat asked bluntly.

McKenzie gave her a look.

"What?" Lilicat said indignantly. "You don't think that's rude, do you?" she demanded of Sharon.

Sharon blushed again. "I don't mind. We moved because my parents just got divorced, and my mom wanted to give us a new start."

"The divorce must have been tough," Mack said sympathetically.

"Yeah . . ." Sharon agreed.

"My parents are divorced, too," said Lilicat. "It happened a long time ago, and I haven't seen my dad much since, but I still wish he were around sometimes."

"I don't miss my father," Sharon said. There was a touch of bitterness in her voice. "I hate him. He ditched my mom for his sexy twenty-one-year-old secretary."

McKenzie and Lilicat gasped in unison.

"Twenty-one! That's like practically our age. Imagine kissing someone as old as your father. Gross," Lilicat said, twisting her mouth in disgust.

"Speaking of gross," Mack said to Sharon, "what do you think of Lakeville High?"

Sharon giggled.

"Who do you have for homeroom?" asked Lilicat.

Sharon covered her face with her hands. When she pulled her hands down, she wore a very stern expression. "All right, everybody just simmer down," she said in a gravelly voice. "Just simmer down *right* now."

"Mrs. Ethelridge!" Mack and Lilicat chorused. Then they both clapped their hands. "Do another one," Lilicat urged.

"All right." Sharon thought a moment, then hunched her shoulders. She made circles with her fingers and put them over her eyes like glasses. "Uh, Sharon?" Her voice was now high and nasal. "You don't know me, but I'm in your biology class with Mr. Kurtz? And I was just wondering if—"

"Neil Buckner," screeched Lilicat. "Don't tell me he's after you already?"

Sharon nodded.

"Poor Neil," said Mack.

"Poor Sharon," said Lilicat. "Neil's not a bad guy. He just never knows when to give up." She got to her feet and started waddling around the room. "Who's this?"

"Mrs. Baumgartner!" yelled McKenzie.

"Oh, that's perfect!" Sharon laughed so hard Mack was afraid she'd choke on her pizza.

Amazing, McKenzie was thinking. This was like—instant chemistry. When Lilicat sat back down, Mack caught her eye. She could tell her friend was thinking the same thing.

Just then, the cheese slid off McKenzie's slice of pizza and onto the white shag carpet. "Whoops," she cried. "Sorry!"

Buttons dove for the food, but Sharon swooped down and got there first. "Don't worry about it," she assured Mack. "I've spilled so much stuff on this rug you could probably cook it and serve it for dinner."

Sharon started wiping the rug with a paper napkin. "Here." She held out another napkin so McKenzie could wipe her hands.

"Thanks." Mack reached out to take the napkin. Her eyes locked with Sharon's.

Those large eyes, perfect, ice blue. So glassy. Like a doll's eyes.

As McKenzie reached for the napkin, she

accidentally grasped Sharon's hand. A surge of pain shot through her.

Mack let out a strangled cry. It felt as if she'd just stuck her hand into an electrical socket.

chapter 2

"Mack? Are you okay?" Lilicat's voice.

"What's going on?!" Sharon's voice.

McKenzie blinked hard but couldn't see. Tried to speak. Couldn't.

"Mack! What is it?!" Lilicat again.

McKenzie yanked her hand away from Sharon's and the pain instantly subsided.

Sharon and Lilicat were both staring at her with frightened faces.

"McKenzie?" Sharon reached out her hand.

McKenzie jerked back. "No!" She took several deep breaths. "I—I'm fine," she stammered. "I just—"

Lilicat draped a hand over McKenzie's shoulder. "What was it, Mack?" she asked gently. "Did you see something? A vision—"

She stopped herself abruptly.

Mack darted a quick look at Sharon. Sharon's eyebrows were lifted in surprise.

"I mean," Lilicat quickly went on, "do you feel all right?"

"Yeah, yeah, it's nothing. I just got a chill." McKenzie gave Lilicat a meaningful look, as if to say, "Watch it."

Lilicat returned the look with one of her own, which Mack easily interpreted as, "I know. Sorry."

"Can I get you something?" Sharon asked, still looking at Mack with undisguised curiosity. "An aspirin? A sweater?"

Had Sharon caught Lilicat's "vision" reference? Mack wasn't sure. But Sharon had to know that something out of the ordinary was in the air.

McKenzie stared down at her hand. This power of hers—sometimes she felt like some kind of witch-weirdo.

"All McKenzie needs is her boyfriend," Lilicat said brightly, trying to change the subject. "She's just used to having Aidan around to keep her warm!"

Sharon looked at McKenzie, who explained, "My boyfriend's away with the school band for two weeks. A few months ago he started playing the tuba, of all things, and joined the band."

"As if he didn't have enough extracurricular activities going already," threw in Lilicat.

"You miss him, huh?" asked Sharon, stretching like a cat.

"Are you kidding? She's climbing the walls," said Lilicat. "And he only left on Wednesday."

Sharon laughed. McKenzie smiled with relief. Everything seemed normal again. But whatever she'd felt when she'd touched Sharon's hand had been anything but normal!

"How about you?" Sharon asked Lilicat. "Do *you* have a boyfriend?"

"Not exactly," Lilicat said. "But I'm working on it."

"Do tell," Sharon prompted.

The three girls instinctively moved closer together, as if someone might be eavesdropping. Lilicat lowered her voice. "Okay. His name is Alec Greene and he's the quarterback for Washington High. I met him at a football game—when I was cheering *against* him. We've only gone out twice, but I'm really crazy about him."

"What does he look like?" Sharon asked.

"Well, he's a definite hunk," Lilicat began. "Tall—"

"I like that," Sharon broke in. "Whenever I go out with short guys, I have to squinch down so they don't feel dwarfed."

"Well, with Alec," Lilicat said, "I've got to stand on my toes when we kiss. But he's worth it," she added dreamily, leaning her head back. "He's the most incredible kisser. He—Ayyy! Yuk!!!" she suddenly shrieked.

As if on cue, Buttons had licked Lilicat right on the lips. Sharon and Mack both fell to the floor, laughing.

"All right," said Lilicat, sitting up straight. "Your turn, Sharon. Who are the cute guys in your life?"

Sharon smiled but didn't answer.

"Well?" prodded Lilicat.

Sharon's smile faded. "I'm not seeing anyone right now."

For a moment McKenzie thought she saw tears in Sharon's large blue eyes, but then she decided it was just a weird reflection from the light.

"So what about back in Cadaret?" Lilicat continued. "Did you leave somebody heartbroken there?"

Sharon shook her head sadly as she spooned a huge lump of ice cream onto Lilicat's plate. "Nope."

"Come on," Lilicat persisted. "We want names, we want all the hot details."

There was something about this topic that McKenzie didn't like. It wasn't just the sadness on Sharon's face—it was a feeling inside McKenzie herself. "This ice cream looks great . . ." she began, trying to change the subject.

Something strange was happening again. Her body didn't feel right. Her feet and hands were going all numb, tingly. Now what would cause *that?*

Lilicat persisted. "Come on, Sharon. I can tell there's something up. Who is he?"

"Maybe she doesn't feel like talking about it," Mack said uncomfortably.

McKenzie didn't feel like talking about it herself. For she was now feeling both pain and fear. In waves. All coming from Sharon! She glanced at her. Sharon's head was down.

McKenzie took a deep breath. Or tried to. She suddenly felt as if there wasn't enough air in the room. As if somehow Sharon was using it all. . . .

"I think Sharon *wants* to tell us," Lilicat plunged on. "She's just a little shy. Right, Sharon?"

Sharon brushed her long blond hair out of her face and tucked it behind an ear. It fell right back. She bit her lip.

McKenzie breathed in long and slow. The fear, the feeling of suffocation—both had passed as quickly as they'd come. But McKenzie could still feel the pain, something dark and hurt, deep inside Sharon. It throbbed in her own brain. What could have happened to hurt her so much? Her parents' divorce? Probably—but there was something else.

"You lost someone you loved, didn't you?" Mack asked quietly. The words had come out before she could stop herself.

Sharon nodded, her head bowed. McKenzie began to reach toward her, to touch her hand— but stopped.

"Oh, no," Lilicat said, flushing hotly. "Me and my big mouth! I'm so sorry!"

"Please," Sharon said, still not looking up. "It's not *your* fault!" She took a couple of quick strides across the room to a box of pink tissues, plucked one out, and blew her nose. "Darn it," she said, "I'm such a fool. Listen, I went through some heavy stuff a few months back, okay?"

"Sure," said Lilicat. "You don't have to talk about it."

"It's crazy," Sharon said, blowing her nose

again. "I've only known you guys an hour and yet I almost feel like I could tell you all about it."

"You could," Lilicat said eagerly.

"Lilicat," Mack rolled her eyes.

Sharon smiled. "That's okay. I promise I'll tell you all about it—some other time. But right now I just feel like having fun." She put on a bright smile and clapped her hands. "So how about we get to work on this fudge ripple!"

Lilicat and Mack both clapped as well. Then they all picked up their spoons and dug in.

"You know what I just realized?" Lilicat said, balancing a load of books in her arms. "I'm a total jerk!"

"What's wrong? What do you mean?" McKenzie asked.

It was Monday afternoon. The bell ending the last period had just rung, and the halls of Lakeville High were filled with noisy students. McKenzie pulled open the combination lock on her locker, #107, and started putting away her textbooks.

"It's Monday. I've got cheerleading practice right now, and a history test tomorrow."

"So?"

"So I haven't even started studying. There's no way I can go to the movies tonight."

"Oh."

The pizza party at Sharon's had ended with Lilicat's suggestion that they all go to the movies the following night—Monday. McKenzie had looked forward to the outing all day.

"I feel rotten about this," Lilicat said. "I mean, I promised her. She's new, she finally makes some friends, and then I cancel. Besides, I really want to get to know her, you know?"

"Don't worry," McKenzie told her. "I'll smooth things over and make you look good. On second thought," she added, "you can do it yourself. Hey, Sharon!" she yelled.

Sharon was closing her locker far down the hall. She waved, flashed a bright grin, and made her way toward them through the crowded hallway.

"Guess what?" Mack greeted her. "Lilicat is bagging the movie tonight because she'd rather study for a history test. Sounds fishy, I know, but that's her story."

"Oh, great," Lilicat said, poking McKenzie in the ribs. "That's really making me look good."

Lilicat apologetically explained the problem to Sharon.

"No problem," Sharon assured her. "We don't need you anyway."

"Bummer!" groaned Lilicat. "I really don't want to miss the fun. Maybe I should just flunk history."

"Forget about it," said Sharon. "We won't have any fun. We'll go to the movie, but I promise we'll hate it, okay?"

Mack and Lilicat laughed with their new friend. It was hard to believe they'd just met her yesterday.

"Don't go to anything I haven't seen," Lilicat ordered as McKenzie and Sharon headed off down the hall.

"We'll see something boring," McKenzie promised. "Like that new Mel Gibson flick."

"Noo!!!"

They could still hear Lilicat moaning as they pushed open the door and walked out into the cold, gray afternoon.

"I'm so glad you're home," Mrs. Gold said as soon as McKenzie opened the front door. "Listen—Blue is sick."

McKenzie nearly dropped her books. "What!"

"Don't worry. It's nothing serious. But he was walking around in circles and acting kind of disoriented, so I took him to the vet."

"The vet?" Poor Blue! He hated doctors as much as she did.

Mrs. Gold went on: "Dr. Grumbach says it's an inner ear infection and he'll have to take antibiotics for the next two weeks. Now I've got to—"

But McKenzie was already across the room, taking the stairs two at a time. She flung open the door to her room and found the cat curled up in his favorite spot on her bed, just below the pillow. "Blue!" she cried.

The old cat opened one eye and raised his head slightly. "Aw, Blue, you sweet thing!" McKenzie stroked his head gently, and was rewarded with a raggedy purr. She could see that the inside of his left ear was stained red with medicine.

Then she remembered Blue rubbing that same ear against her knee last night.

"I'll be right back," McKenzie assured Blue. She went out into the hall and followed the phone cord into Jimmy's room, where she retrieved the phone from under a pile of dirty laundry and football cards. She had to call information to get Sharon's number. Sharon answered after one ring.

"Listen," Mack said, "I'm really sorry to do this, but my cat is sick and . . . I don't know,

I just feel I should stay home tonight. Let's do the movie tomorrow or Wednesday."

There was a long moment of silence at the other end of the line. "That way Lilicat can join us too," McKenzie offered.

Sharon sighed loudly. "But you promised!"

"I know," said McKenzie, taken aback. "But I didn't know that Blue—"

"First Lilicat backs out, and now you! Is your cat *really* sick?"

"You think I'd make that up?" McKenzie asked.

"I don't know. It sounds like you never wanted to go to the movies with me in the first place!"

McKenzie stared at the phone in disbelief. "Sharon, that isn't true, I promise."

"You *promise*?" said Sharon, her voice rising. "You just broke a promise. Why should I believe this one?" And before McKenzie had a chance to reply, Sharon hung up.

McKenzie stood in the hallway, holding the phone, amazed. Talk about overreacting!

Then she remembered how excited Sharon had been to make some friends. She remembered the way Sharon's mom had practically ignored her, wrapped up in her own world, her own problems. She remembered the sadness she felt from Sharon. Mack felt a pang of sympathy and guilt. Had she really done something terrible by canceling the movie date? It *was* last-minute. And her excuse *had* sounded kind of lame. But wouldn't Sharon have done the same thing if Buttons had gotten sick?

She tried to call Sharon back but no one picked up. Was she refusing to answer?

"Blue," McKenzie told the cat as she returned to her room, "you just got me in trouble." She walked over to the bed and patted him gently. Blue closed his eyes in pleasure.

"To make up for it, you'll just have to get better right away," Mack whispered.

McKenzie smiled as Blue closed his eyes. "Good idea," she said. "Sleep it off." She got up off the bed lightly, careful not to disturb him, and crossed to her desk. Opening the top drawer, she felt along the underside of the desktop. She pulled out the tiny gold key she had taped there, then bent down and pulled out the desk itself. She reached in back to open the secret drawer and remove her diary.

Someone watching this would probably think I'm totally paranoid, Mack thought. But her diary was one of the few places where she felt totally free to unwind, free to talk about anything—including her own unusual powers. She hated to think what would happen if this diary ever fell into the wrong hands. Jimmy's, for instance.

McKenzie shuddered. Then she unlocked the diary and flipped through the pages until she came to a blank.

"Monday, December 3, 4:30 p.m.," she wrote. "I just got home from school, and Blue is sick. It's scary. He *is* getting old, after all."

She paused for a moment, feeling her eyes suddenly begin to water. She turned to look at Blue's dear face, resting on his paws. His eyes were shut; he was still snoring. "I just can't imagine life without old Blue," she wrote.

She turned the page and continued:

Lilicat and I have made a new friend. Her name is Sharon Roderick, and she's funny and pretty, with long blond hair and this kind of sultry voice. I really like her, but something keeps bothering me about her. Not just today's phone call. Last night, I had this very strange reaction when we touched. And I get this feeling of sadness and fear from her. I hope I'm way off on this one, but I'm pretty sure something weird is going on with her. She got kind of upset last night when Lilicat asked her if she had a boyfriend . . . and then tonight.

The doorbell rang just as McKenzie finished writing the final *t*. She heard her mom yell, "I'll get it." Then muffled voices, her mom's and—Sharon's.

McKenzie's first feeling was panic. Had Sharon come over to chew her out for breaking their date?

This was crazy. Was she actually scared of this girl?

She heard footsteps climbing the stairs. Then there was a soft knock at her door. McKenzie tossed the diary into her desk drawer and closed it tightly.

"Come in," she called, making an effort to sound warm and welcoming.

McKenzie's mother opened the door and entered. Mack waited for Sharon to follow her into the room, but Mrs. Gold was alone. "A friend of yours—Sharon—just stopped by," she said.

"She's gone?" McKenzie asked, surprised.

"Yes, I invited her up, but she didn't want to bother you," Mrs. Gold said. "She asked me to give you this."

Mrs. Gold handed McKenzie a large card that appeared to be homemade. On the front was a picture of a cat with a thermometer in its mouth.

The mercury was blue, and the caption read, "Don't Be Blue!" Inside was a picture of the same cat, dancing. "Feel better soon!" read the caption. Underneath that, Sharon had written, "Sorry I was so uptight on the phone!" And taped underneath *that* was a plastic pouch of catnip.

"That's so sweet," her mom said when McKenzie showed her the card.

"I know," McKenzie agreed. Now she felt doubly bad about having canceled the movie date.

"She seems like a very nice girl. So pretty," her mom added. "Is she new in town?"

"Yeah."

"Well." Mrs. Gold reached over and patted the sleeping cat. "Poor old Blue." She glanced at the pile of laundry in the corner.

She and her mother seemed to argue more about the laundry than anything else. "Tomorrow, I promise," McKenzie said quickly.

Mrs. Gold rolled her eyes and headed back downstairs. "No time like the present," she called over her shoulder.

I guess I *should* do a wash, McKenzie thought. And I *shouldn't* take that phone thing too seriously. Sharon must really have been looking forward to the movies. She must really like me and Lilicat.

Well, that was fine, because she and Lilicat really liked Sharon.

Sharon didn't have to worry. She *had* made two new friends.

chapter 3

The next night, the Gold phone rang during dinner. "I bet it's lover boy," sang Jimmy as Mrs. Gold went to answer it.

A minute later, she returned to the table. "It's for you," she said, tousling McKenzie's hair.

"Told you so!" Jimmy smirked.

McKenzie blushed and headed for the phone. Her heart had started to race. She felt silly; Aidan had only been away for four days. But it was the longest they'd ever been separated.

"Hello?" she said breathlessly into the phone.

"Hi," said a girl's voice.

"Sharon!" exclaimed McKenzie, trying to mask her disappointment.

"I just wanted to see how Blue was doing."

"He seems okay," Mack said. "You're sweet to call."

McKenzie had already thanked Sharon for the card—twice. Once when they rode on the bus together to school. Again when Sharon joined her and Lilicat for lunch. Now she wondered if she should thank her a third time, but that seemed ridiculous.

"Listen," Mack said, "we're kind of in the middle of dinner. Can I call you back in an hour or so?"

"Sure," Sharon said quickly, and hung up.

McKenzie hoped she hadn't hurt Sharon's feelings. But they *were* eating dinner. Oh, well, she thought, I'll call her back later.

Twenty minutes later, the phone rang. This time it's *got* to be Aidan, McKenzie told herself, pouncing on the phone.

"Is this a better time?" Sharon asked.

"Much better," McKenzie said.

"I don't really have much to say, I'm just calling to chat," Sharon said. But then she proceeded to tell McKenzie about her day. And McKenzie found herself chatting about *her* day.

"Oh, God, I guess I really *did* have a lot to say," Sharon admitted half an hour later. "Actually, I was just feeling kind of lonesome. Sorry. I didn't mean to chew your ear off." She laughed. "If Mrs. Ethelridge were here she'd say"—Sharon lowered her voice—" 'Sharon, zip that lip!' "

McKenzie laughed. Sharon really was funny sometimes—and easy to talk to.

When McKenzie finally got off the phone she checked her watch. She wondered if Aidan had been trying to reach her.

"Aidan!" she answered when the phone rang again at ten.

"It's only me," Sharon said. "Were you expecting a call from Aidan?"

"Constantly."

Sharon laughed. "I just can't get myself to do my homework," she complained. "Thought I'd take a break."

"Sharon," McKenzie said. "I really am expecting Aidan to call. I want to keep the line open. We don't have call-waiting."

"You should get it—it's really great. Oh, wait—the line, right? I'm sorry," said Sharon. "I'll get off right now." She hung up the phone without another word.

Now Aidan better call, McKenzie thought. She stared at the phone, willing it to ring. But it didn't.

The next night, Wednesday, Sharon called four times. McKenzie liked Sharon, but her calls were getting to be a bit too much. McKenzie knew she had to tell her, but every time she started to say something she thought about Sharon's sadness. Whatever had happened to her back in Cadaret had left her in need of friends. So what if she calls too much. It seemed so petty to complain about it. Besides, Mack really did want to get to know her better.

Then, on Thursday night, the phone rang just as McKenzie was getting ready for bed. If this isn't Aidan, she told herself, I'll . . . I don't know what.

"It's me," Lilicat said.

"Oh."

"Well, don't sound so excited."

"I was hoping you were Aidan."

"Sorry to disappoint you," Lilicat said dryly.

"It's not that," McKenzie said. "It's just that Sharon's called twice already."

"That girl," Lilicat said happily. "I have to say, Sharon is the nicest person I've met in ages. Don't you just love her?"

"Uh-huh," McKenzie forced herself to agree.

"I told you about shopping for makeup with her, didn't I?"

"No."

"Yesterday, we went shopping for some eye shadow. We ended up having this great talk about divorce and what it does to you and all. I told her things I've never told anyone."

McKenzie couldn't help feeling a pang of jealousy. Things Lilicat had never told *anyone*. They were supposed to tell each other *everything,* weren't they? "Oh?" she said.

"Yeah," said Lilicat. "It just felt good to talk to someone who's been through the same thing."

"I guess," McKenzie agreed, trying not to sound hurt.

"Oh, and wait till you hear what she did today," Lilicat rushed on. "You know how much trouble I was having thinking up an idea for my English essay? Well, when I got home, Sharon had dropped off this list of ten possible ideas. I used one of them, and I think it turned out pretty good."

"Pretty well," corrected McKenzie.

"All right," Lilicat said, "so I won't get an *A*. But wasn't that sweet of her?"

"Uh-huh."

"Okay, Mack. What's going on?" Lilicat asked. "*Something's* wrong. I can tell."

"You're a real mind reader," Mack said.

"Takes one to know one."

McKenzie sighed. "Something *is* bothering me—about Sharon."

There was a worried silence at the other end. "What is it?" Lilicat asked finally.

"I wish I knew," McKenzie said. "I'm not real clear on this. But I go back and forth about her. I really like her, and yet sometimes she just gets on my nerves."

"Why?" asked Lilicat. "What do you mean?"

"I don't know," McKenzie said again. "I get this feeling that something's not right with her—with us. It's hard to explain."

There was another long pause. Then Lilicat said softly, "Does it have something to do with me? Are you upset because I've started spending time with her alone?"

"No, that's not it," McKenzie insisted.

"Are you sure?"

"Lilicat—listen, if there's one part of the future that I know I can predict, it's that . . . well, you and I are going to be friends—forever."

"That proves you're psychic," Lilicat agreed happily. "So . . . stop worrying about Sharon, okay?"

"Wait a minute," McKenzie said. "That really isn't what's bothering me."

"Then what?"

"I don't know. She calls here a lot," McKenzie finished lamely.

"So? That's great. She calls me a lot, too. I call her a lot. I think this is fabulous."

"I know, but don't you worry she might be a little . . . I don't know . . . clingy?"

"*Sharon?* Clingy?" said Lilicat, incredulous. "Okay, she strikes me as kind of secretive, mysterious maybe. But clingy? No way. I wish I knew what really happened to her back in Cadaret, though, don't you? I bet it has something to do with a guy. It must be something really bad if she doesn't want to talk about it."

"Yeah, I wish she would tell us. Maybe that's part of my problem. I'm like running out of things to say to her," McKenzie said. "I mean, you eat lunch with her every day. She rides next to me on the bus every morning. And yet there's so much about her we don't know."

"Hey," said Lilicat. "Don't be too hard on her. From what she was telling me about this divorce thing—her story sounds a lot worse than mine. Plus she's had to leave all her friends and move to a new school. . . . She must feel like her whole world is falling apart. You just don't know how hard it can be."

McKenzie knew Lilicat was right. It was probably the divorce that was making Sharon seem so sad. But still the bad feeling she had about Sharon wouldn't go away. For once, she thought, it would be nice to be wrong.

When the phone rang on Sunday, McKenzie answered warily.

"Hey," said a familiar male voice.

"Aidan! How are you? Where are you? How's it going?"

His answers came as quickly as her questions: "Great!" "Detroit!" "Fantastic!" He was bubbling over with enthusiasm about his trip.

"I'm not sure I like you having such a good time," McKenzie said, only half-kidding.

"Why not?" Aidan sounded genuinely mystified.

"Because you're supposed to be missing me too much to enjoy yourself."

"Oh." He laughed. "Well I do—I am—I miss you like crazy!"

"It may be too late for that," McKenzie said. "Then again, you might try giving me some details—maybe that will do the trick."

"Well, for starters, I've been dreaming about you every night."

"That's better."

"The guys in the band are getting sick of hearing me talk about you all the time. They've been threatening to ship me home to you."

"Now you're talking!"

"And . . ." Aidan went on. By the time he was through, Mack was feeling better than she had since he'd gone.

"I gotta go," Aidan said finally. "This is costing a fortune."

"It's worth every penny. Come back tomorrow," she begged.

"I'll be home on Tuesday," he promised. "Which reminds me. I have a favor to ask. My mom's going to be at work when the bus comes in. Any chance you could pick me up?"

"None. But I'll be there."

After telling her exactly when and where to meet him, Aidan said, "Okay, there's about six people waiting to use the phone. I gotta run." And he was gone.

McKenzie felt a sudden rush of loneliness. She quickly picked up the phone again. She called Lilicat and asked her if she wanted to come over and study for their math test. She was about to add, "Just the two of us this time, okay?"

But Lilicat immediately said, "Hold on. . . . You want to go to Mack's to do some studying?"

A soft, throaty voice answered, "Sure."

"Great," Lilicat exclaimed happily. "Sharon's coming too," she added.

McKenzie stayed after school on Monday to work on her bimonthly column at the *Guardian* office.

She smiled when she heard a knock at the door. The smile faded when she saw who it was.

"Hi," said Sharon, walking in with her usual grin and one hand behind her back. She quickly brought the hand forward, holding it out to McKenzie. In her hand was a luscious-looking muffin. "It's banana-peanut-butter-chip. I baked it myself." And putting a hand up to the side of her mouth as if imparting a big secret, she whispered, "From a mix."

"Wow," said McKenzie. "Thanks." She took a bite and couldn't help smiling. "This is fantastic!"

"Thanks," said Sharon, blushing. "So listen, I was thinking, since I'm new, I ought to join some activities or something, right? That way, I'll meet lots of other kids. I don't want you and Lilicat getting sick of me."

"We're not sick of you," McKenzie assured her, almost meaning it at that moment. "But sure, joining a club is a great idea. What about the hockey team? Didn't you play field hockey at your old school?"

"Well, yes," said Sharon slowly. "How did you know that?"

McKenzie shrugged. It had simply popped into her head, as a fact that she knew. "You must have told me about it at some point."

"No," Sharon said. "I'm sure I never mentioned it."

McKenzie hesitated. She couldn't remember whether Sharon had mentioned it or not. Sometimes things like this just occurred to McKenzie. It was part of her powers—powers she didn't want Sharon to know anything about. "Sharon, I'm sure you must have told me. How else would I know?"

Sharon gave her a funny look. "I don't know," she said in a strange voice. "But I know I never told you."

There was an uncomfortable silence. McKenzie broke it.

"Well, if you don't want to play hockey, what else are you interested in?"

"Well, I've always been interested in writing," Sharon said. Her manner was suddenly friendly again. She spread her arms wide. "Meet your new *Guardian* volunteer."

It took McKenzie a couple of seconds before she could plaster a pleased smile on her face. There went her last refuge.

That night, Sharon called twice before seven-thirty. The third time the phone rang, McKenzie picked it up in exasperation and said, "Hi, Sharon."

"You knew it was me!" Sharon cried, sounding pleased.

"Just a wild guess," said McKenzie. "So what's up?"

"Nothing," Sharon said with a nervous laugh. "I just wanted to chat."

McKenzie shook her head in amazement. How much chatting could two people do? And what could they chat about? They saw each other six times a day in school.

After an awkward silence, Sharon finally said, "Is this a bad time?"

"No, not really," McKenzie said. But what she felt like saying was, "You called *me,* remember? *You* talk." Instead, she forced herself to ask, "What's on your mind?"

"There's something I want to tell you," Sharon began. Then she paused again.

"What?" McKenzie prompted.

"Maybe now's not a good time to go into it," Sharon said. "I get the feeling you're busy or something."

"Well . . ." McKenzie could feel another guilt attack coming on, but she said, "I *was* in the middle of my trig homework. I don't know about you, but math is really torture for me."

"Fine. 'Bye," said Sharon abruptly. The line clicked dead.

McKenzie held the phone to her ear for a moment, her finger poised over the touch-tone buttons, ready to call Sharon back. Finally, she hung up, too. She'd call later—when she was in a better mood.

McKenzie concentrated on the problems before her, blinking her eyes and willing herself to continue. She was on the verge of solving the next problem when the phone rang jarringly. She snatched up the receiver. "Hello?"

"I feel *so* sorry for her," Lilicat began.

"Who, Sharon? Why?" asked McKenzie, but she felt as if somehow, she already knew the answer.

"Listen to this," Lilicat continued. "Remember when we first met her? How you felt that pain when you touched her hand and she promised she'd tell us sometime about how she lost somebody? Well, she just told me the whole awful story."

"What happened?" McKenzie asked.

"She had this boyfriend, Brad," Lilicat explained. "This *fantastic* guy, okay? They were totally in love, even talked about getting married someday. Well, this summer he died in a car accident. He was eighteen years old!"

McKenzie didn't say a word. She felt as if someone had just punched her in the stomach.

"How did it happen?" she burst out. "Was he driving? Was she in the car?"

Lilicat cut her off. "She didn't give me any of those details. All I know is Brad was killed. And you know what they found in his pocket?" Lilicat didn't wait for an answer. "His class ring—wrapped up like a gift. He was all set to give it to Sharon that night. Sharon said he'd beem hinting about it all week, that he wanted to give her something special. Can you believe that? Isn't that the absolute worst? I mean, can you imagine if something like that happened to you? How would you ever go on? I wouldn't. I would just die, on the spot."

McKenzie closed her eyes as a tremendous wave of remorse flooded through her. Sharon had called to talk to her, to unburden herself, and she hadn't even been willing to listen.

"So that's what she wanted to talk about," McKenzie mumbled.

"Huh? What do you mean?" Lilicat asked.

"She called here too. I'm afraid that I was a little . . ."

"A little what?"

"I don't know. Rude, I guess," McKenzie said. It embarrassed her to say the word.

Lilicat's response didn't help. "You were rude to *Sharon?* Why Sharon, of all people?"

"You're right," sighed McKenzie, rubbing her temples with her free hand. "I didn't *mean* to be mean. I've just been feeling a little down lately. Blue is still sick, and Aidan's away, and . . . Oh, I don't know—"

"Okay, okay," Lilicat cut her off. "That's enough excuses. But can you imagine? He died with her ring in his pocket!"

With her ring in his pocket. The words hung in the air even after McKenzie got off the phone. They seemed to accuse her. She called Sharon back, but Mrs. Roderick answered and said she'd gone to bed.

I bet she went to bed upset, McKenzie chided herself.

The next morning, McKenzie grabbed a chocolate-chip cookie out of the cookie jar and wrapped it in a napkin to give to Sharon. Then she rushed out the door just as the school bus turned down the street.

Lumpy Johnson waved to her as she got on. She waved back but sat by herself so she could save a seat for Sharon. She looked out the window, peering up ahead at the turnoff to Oak Lawn. Every morning, Sharon waited at that corner.

Every morning except this one.

The bus was getting closer, picking up speed.

McKenzie craned her neck to look down Oak
Lawn as they passed by, expecting to see Sharon
coming on the run.

The street was deserted. McKenzie suddenly
got a sickening feeling. Something was terribly
wrong. It was so weird—she felt like her insides
were being crushed. Where was Sharon? Was
she okay?

Then McKenzie saw her. Sharon was running
through a stand of trees beside the road. She
had taken a shortcut.

McKenzie glanced frantically at the bus driver.
He wasn't going to stop. He never stopped
unless the person was at the arranged stop.
Never.

The bus took the corner fast.

Suddenly Mack opened her mouth to scream
as—

Sharon darted out, right into the middle of
the road.

The bus hurtled toward her.

chapter 4

The brakes screeched and whined as the bus jerked to a stop.

Everyone rocked violently forward, then back. Kids cried out in fear and pain.

McKenzie looked around wildly. She saw Lumpy Johnson holding his head. She peered out the window, but she couldn't see Sharon!

The driver pulled open the doors and stomped off the bus. Soon, McKenzie and the other students could hear him yelling at someone. She couldn't hear it all, but at least it meant that Sharon was alive.

When the driver got back on the bus, he was flushed with anger. Sharon was right behind him, looking paler than usual, her blue eyes steady but blank. No one said a word to her as she marched down the aisle and slipped into the seat beside McKenzie.

"Looks like everyone's giving me the silent treatment," Sharon said.

"Are you crazy?" McKenzie blurted out before she could stop herself. "You could have gotten yourself killed!"

"Please," said Sharon. "I already heard that from the driver."

"Well, you could have. Not to mention the rest of us!"

"If you ask me," Sharon said, twisting around in her seat, "the bus driver's the one who's crazy. Did you hear him screaming? You'd think I'd been hit. You saw it, didn't you? He didn't even come that close to me! He couldn't have hit me." Then, turning back to McKenzie, she said, "Does he always overreact this way?"

Okay, McKenzie told herself. Take deep breaths. Try to calm down.

"And I think you're overreacting a little bit too," Sharon said.

McKenzie stared at her in disbelief, then looked away. Why was Sharon acting this way? And why would she have put herself in such danger?

"I really needed to make the bus," Sharon added, as if answering McKenzie's unspoken question. "I've already been late twice. Besides"—she pinned Mack with her big blue eyes—"I like riding to school with you."

McKenzie looked away. *Unreal* was the word that came to mind. Sharon chattered on for most of the ride, but McKenzie couldn't bring herself to say much more than "uh-huh" and "yeah."

McKenzie breathed a sigh of relief when the bus swung into the parking lot in front of the dull tan brick buildings that were Lakeville High.

Sharon stood next to McKenzie as they got off the bus. "Excuse me," Mack said, pulling away. "Are you okay?" she asked Lumpy, who had stopped several feet away.

Lumpy blinked several times and shook his head. "I feel a little dizzy," he admitted.

She took his arm. "You got a pretty bad knock." McKenzie shot a worried look back at Sharon. "Come on. I'll take you to the nurse."

After a quick examination, the school nurse gave Lumpy an ice pack and declared, "He looks fine to me, but I'm afraid he's going to have a decent-sized lump."

"A lump for Lumpy," said McKenzie, patting his shoulder. She grinned at him.

But inside, she was still worried. And when she passed Lilicat in the hall on the way to first period, she said, "I really have to talk to you—alone—today. How about lunch?"

"I'll tell Sharon," Lilicat promised, heading off down the hall.

McKenzie ran after her. "Wait a minute. Didn't you hear what I said? *Alone.* That means me and you. Not Sharon." And when she saw the surprised look in her friend's eyes, she added, "Sorry. I didn't mean to snap at you. But we've really got to talk."

"Okay," said Lilicat, looking puzzled. "I guess we can tell her to sit somewhere else today, but that'll be kind of awkward, don't you think?"

"I've got a better idea," said McKenzie. "Did you bring your lunch?" Lilicat nodded. "Good. The band rehearsal room isn't locked. And I know it'll be empty, since the band's at the competition."

Brightening, Lilicat gave McKenzie a thumbs-up sign. "I'll be there."

When the lunch bell rang, McKenzie hurried to her locker, grabbed her lunch bag, and headed for the rehearsal room. She fully expected Sharon to turn up at any moment.

This is crazy, she thought. Sharon had her hiding in her own school.

She considered stopping at the cafeteria to

buy a drink, but she didn't want to risk running into Sharon and having to explain why she wasn't eating with her. Besides, she didn't want to waste a minute of her time with Lilicat. Glancing back over her shoulder, she pushed open the door to the music room.

Her face lit up at the sight of Lilicat, sitting in front of a music stand with a half-eaten tuna sandwich resting on a napkin on her lap. Lilicat gave McKenzie a sheepish grin. "Couldn't wait," she explained. "I was starving."

McKenzie pulled up a chair across from Lilicat. The two girls talked while Mack spread out her own lunch.

"So what happened on the bus this morning?" Lilicat asked. "I heard something about the driver almost running over Sharon."

McKenzie rubbed her face with both hands. Now that she and Lilicat were actually alone, she wasn't sure what to say. "Look," she began. "I'm getting more and more worried about Sha—"

The fire alarm blasted in their ears, drowning out McKenzie's last words.

"Oh, no," groaned McKenzie. Their private lunch was going to be ruined—by a fire drill, of all things.

"It'll probably stop," Lilicat shouted over the noise. "They never have fire drills during lunch. Hey, maybe it's a real fire! . . ."

It didn't stop.

"Well," Lilicat yelled, gathering her lunch, "I guess we'd better get moving."

Out in the parking lot, the students were gathering by homeroom. Kids peered all around at the school buildings. No sign of smoke anywhere. And certainly no heat. It was a freezing day, and without their jackets, everyone was soon shivering in the cold.

Suddenly, a figure broke through the crowd and grabbed McKenzie's arm.

"Where *were* you guys?" Sharon asked. "I couldn't find you in the lunchroom or in study hall or anywhere."

"We were hanging out in the band room," said Lilicat. "Can you believe they're having a fire drill on the coldest day of the year? What are they trying to do to us?"

"They're *not* having a fire drill," said Sharon, a sly smile curling her lips. She started giggling uncontrollably.

McKenzie gave her a worried look, remembering how strange Sharon had acted on the bus that morning. "What do you mean?" she asked.

But she had a sinking feeling that she already
knew the answer.

"*I* pulled the alarm," Sharon said simply.
"Hey, I had to find you guys, didn't I? I don't
have anyone else to eat with."

chapter 5

"Sharon, are you kidding?" McKenzie said. "Did you really pull the alarm? Why would you do such a crazy thing?"

Sharon looked at McKenzie in amazement, her blue eyes rounder than ever. For a moment, she just stared. Then her eyes filled with tears and she turned quickly away.

"Hold on, Mack," said Lilicat. "You don't have to get mad . . ."

"Lilicat, you didn't see what happened on the bus this morning!" Mack broke in. "Sharon could have been killed, Lumpy bashed his head . . ."

"I won't do anything like this again," said

Sharon quietly. "I promise. I just panicked when you weren't there . . ."

"All right, people," Mr. Cartwright's voice boomed through his megaphone. "False alarm. Everyone back inside."

"I really am sorry," Sharon continued. "But I don't see why you're so upset. McKenzie, you knew there wasn't a real fire, didn't you? You know all kinds of things, you know, before other people do. . . ."

McKenzie's mouth dropped open as Sharon's voice trailed off insinuatingly.

"Let's go eat," Lilicat said quickly. "I'm going to die if I don't finish my tuna sandwich."

"Good idea," said Sharon. "I'm starving."

"I've gotta check something at the paper," said Mack. "I'll see you guys later." And without another word, she headed off for the library—to be alone.

McKenzie caught up with Lilicat in the crowded hall after fourth period. "Why did you run off like that at lunchtime?" Lilicat asked her.

"I just needed to get away," said McKenzie. "Lilicat, I'm *really* worried about Sharon. She's much too dependent on us. This fire alarm thing was really weird. You have to admit that."

"Yeah, it was strange," said Lilicat. She shrugged. "Everybody gets a little weird sometimes."

"It's not just that," said McKenzie uncomfortably. "I'm starting to wonder—"

"Wonder what?"

"Lilicat," McKenzie said, "did you tell Sharon anything?"

"Anything about what?"

"About me. About—you know—the visions . . ."

"Of course not," Lilicat said. "I promised you I'd never tell anyone, and I never will."

McKenzie looked down at her feet. She didn't know how to say what she was thinking without hurting Lilicat's feelings. But Lilicat must have guessed.

"Mack, I'm really sorry about the other night at Sharon's. I know I almost blew it when I said that thing about visions. It just slipped out—I couldn't help it. I'm sure she had no idea what I was talking about. I mean, how could anybody guess that?"

"I don't know," McKenzie said. "But I think she has. The way she made that crack about me knowing there wasn't a fire. . . . And I'm afraid I let something slip out myself. I told her I knew she played field hockey at her old school, but she claims she's never mentioned it. I don't know how I knew that, but it seemed to make her suspicious."

"Don't be silly. All she knows is that you're a great friend—and maybe just a little whacked sometimes," Lilicat teased.

McKenzie smiled, then quickened her pace as a man's voice called out, "Any day now." Mr. Rodman was waiting for them a few feet down the hall in the open door of his classroom. "Or perhaps you'd rather make up the class in detention?" he said sternly.

McKenzie tried to concentrate on trigonometry, but she couldn't get Sharon out of her mind. And she suddenly felt very trapped. How far would Sharon's dependency on her and Lilicat go? She'd already done some pretty dangerous things. What would she do next?

After math, McKenzie was making her way through the jostling mass of students, heading for biology, when a too-familiar voice called out, "Hey, Mack, wait up!"

Sharon.

McKenzie pretended not to hear and hooked a quick left. But Sharon managed to catch up anyway.

"Listen, McKenzie. I'm sorry about everything. I didn't mean any harm. I thought you'd get a kick out of the fire drill. I just want you guys to be my friends, that's all."

McKenzie didn't answer. She felt bad for Sharon. Her insecurity was really painful.

"I really am sorry," Sharon said. She lowered her head, biting her lip. Her straight blond hair fell in a slash across her face. "Let me make it up to you," she began, looking up with a sad smile. "How about we go out for ice cream tonight—on me?"

"It's okay, Sharon. You don't have to take me out. I'm busy tonight, anyway."

"Oh, that's right," Sharon nodded. "Lilicat told me. Aidan's coming back today."

"Yeah. Just don't worry so much, okay?"

Sharon beamed. It took so little make her happy. "Okay."

"Well . . ." McKenzie said, searching for a graceful way to end the conversation.

But Sharon just kept staring at her.

"Hey," Sharon said. "Why don't we get together, the four of us? I'd love to meet this boyfriend of yours."

Any good feelings McKenzie had for Sharon quickly vanished. What was wrong with her? McKenzie hadn't seen Aidan in almost two weeks. The last thing she wanted was to get together in a group.

"You want to be alone, don't you?" Sharon went on, reading her expression. "Sorry, I'm doing it again, aren't I? Pushing too hard."

McKenzie blushed. "That's okay. We'll do it some other time," she promised. "Well . . . see you later." She started backing away, waiting for Sharon's good-bye.

But the good-bye didn't come. Sharon was already halfway down the hall.

"Gross," Jimmy said, when McKenzie came into the kitchen late that afternoon. "What did you do to your lips?"

"Ever hear of lipstick?"

The phone rang before he could answer. McKenzie started. Her first thought was to make Jimmy answer, in case it was Sharon, but that seemed too silly. She grabbed the receiver on the second ring. "Hello?"

It was her mother. "The Shanleys have decided they *must* see the Potter house one more time and right away," Mrs. Gold told her. "So it looks as if I'm going to be a little late."

"So am I," McKenzie said. "I'm picking Aidan up at school."

"Is Daddy home yet?"

McKenzie glanced out the kitchen window. When he wasn't behind the counter of the hardware store he owned in town, he was most often in his basement workroom, constructing his aluminum sculptures. Right now he was outside, erecting his latest creation: *Adam and Eve.*

"He's here," McKenzie said.

"Has he put the fig leaves on yet?" Mrs. Gold asked hopefully.

"I don't know, I'm afraid to look."

When she hung up, Jimmy flashed her a knowing grin. "So that's what the lipstick is for. Careful you don't get it all over Aidan when you kiss him hello," he said, puckering his lips and making loud smacking noises as Mack grabbed her coat and hurried out the door.

McKenzie got to the school gym about fifteen minutes early. And the bus was late. She stood waiting in the middle of a crowd of parents. For once, she had no problem putting Sharon out of her mind. All she could think of was Aidan. She'd never been so eager to see anyone in her entire life.

"There it is," said a redheaded girl McKenzie recognized from school. As the bus pulled into the gym parking lot, McKenzie glimpsed several familiar faces, pressed against the glass. Almost immediately, a line of students, many carrying instrument cases, started filing off.

McKenzie waited anxiously. A large black tuba case emerged from the bus, but it was carried by a thin, nerdy-looking kid wearing round, black-rimmed glasses.

Then came another tuba case. And this one was carried by a tall, handsome boy with rumpled sandy hair.

"Aidan!" McKenzie shouted, even though she was only a few feet away.

Aidan waved to her, and a sunny smile burst across his face. He took three giant steps, carefully put down his tuba, then lifted her into the air. He just stood there, hugging her for a long time. McKenzie could tell that he had missed her, too, and she couldn't help feeling glad.

They were drifting toward Mack's car now, fighting over Aidan's suitcase. Aidan won. He always insisted on carrying everything.

"Tell me all about it," McKenzie demanded as soon as they pulled out of the school parking lot.

Aidan obeyed, describing his trip in detail, right down to the band's third-place finish in the national playoffs.

He'd barely finished the story when they reached his house. And then his brothers made him tell the whole thing all over again.

But finally, Mack and Aidan were alone in Aidan's room.

"Hey," Aidan said, brushing her hair away from her face. "There's something I haven't told you yet."

"I doubt it," teased McKenzie. "I'm sure you told me *everything*. Twice."

"Not about the trip," said Aidan seriously.

"Is there another subject?" McKenzie was feeling nervous again, shy—as if this were their first date!

"I haven't told you how much I missed you," Aidan said softly.

All tension flowed out of her with a rush. Then Aidan's lips were on hers; their heads tilted, their mouths and bodies pressed together.

"Whew," Aidan said, pulling back. "I stink."

McKenzie giggled. "Talk about a mood breaker."

Aidan raised one arm, sniffed, and made a face. "Would you mind hanging out while I pop into the shower? I want to take you to Uncle John's for a banana split. Then, after dessert, I thought we'd have a little dinner at Burger Brew. And maybe a movie. What do you say?"

"I've gotta tell my parents, but—" McKenzie grinned widely—"I say yes!"

Aidan grabbed a blue towel that was draped over his dresser and ducked into the bathroom. With a loud sigh of contentment, McKenzie plopped down on his bed. Folding her hands behind her neck and crossing her legs, she stared at the model airplanes hanging from the ceiling. She closed her eyes and imagined that she was a genie flying through the sky on a magic carpet. A feeling of peace settled over her. For the first time in days, she was totally relaxed.

Aidan was singing a marching tune in the shower—at least it *sounded* like a marching tune. These days, he only sang the "oompah, oom-pah" tuba part. She smiled. The sound of the drumming water and Aidan's singing soothed her. He's back! she told herself several times. Now everything would go back to normal—it just had to.

But suddenly McKenzie's good feeling began to fade. The muscles in her shoulders and neck tensed up. She tried to reach up and rub her neck, but she couldn't seem to make her arm move.

Sharon's craziness must be rubbing off on me, McKenzie thought.

She tried again to move her arm. She couldn't lift it. She began to panic. She tried to move her other arm, but it seemed to be glued to her side. She tried to move her legs. She could bend her knees, but she couldn't get her ankles apart.

The model airplanes swayed back and forth

as she twisted from side to side. The walls seemed to close in on her. She wanted to push them away to protect herself, but she couldn't lift her arms. The walls moved in closer and closer. She felt suffocated, trapped. She couldn't breathe! What was happening to her? Why couldn't she move?

She heaved her body to the left with all her might—

And landed on the floor with a clunk. She gasped for breath. For the moment, she didn't mind having fallen; she was just happy to be able to breathe freely again. The suffocating feeling had vanished, as suddenly as it had arrived. She was back in Aidan's room and everything was okay.

Aidan's curious face appeared above hers. He was wearing crisp new jeans and a white T-shirt. A drop of water fell from his wet hair and hit her cheek.

"Looking for something?" he joked.

She carefully tried to lift her right arm. It moved easily. She rubbed her head and smiled tentatively at him.

"Are you okay?" he asked her, seriously now.

She nodded and sat up. Her legs were working normally again, too. What had just happened to her? She had felt trapped on the bed, paralyzed—until she had fallen and broken the spell. What did it mean?

"Mack?"

She stood up and said, "I'll explain in the car." Whatever had just happened to her, it meant something. She had a terrible feeling that it was a bad omen. But for now she was safe with Aidan, and that was all she cared about.

"Two splits?" Dottie, the waitress, greeted them when they slid into a window booth at Uncle John's half an hour later.

"How did you guess?" Aidan asked with a smile. Then he leaned across the table and took both of McKenzie's hands in his. "I'm thinking of cutting back on some of my after-school activities."

A slow smile spread across McKenzie's face. "Do you mean it?" she asked eagerly.

"Absolutely." Aidan puckered his lips and blew out noisily. "Sorry," he said. "That's good tuba practice. Mr. Karlson thinks I have some real potential as a tuba player. But he suggested I cut down on some of my other activities so I can practice more."

McKenzie laughed.

"What are you laughing about?" Aidan asked.

"Nothing. For a moment I thought you were

going to cut down on your activities because
you already have things scheduled eight days a
week. I should know you better than that!"

"Hey," Aidan said, his gray eyes searching
her green ones. He shook his head. "You know
me. But what about you? I'm just so wired
from the trip. I haven't asked you one question
about you. Well, that's going to stop right now."
He smiled slyly. "What do *you* think about me?"

McKenzie couldn't help laughing.

"Hey," Aidan said again. He stretched across
the table to kiss her. "Seriously, what's been
going on? How've you been?"

Where to begin? When she thought about it,
it didn't really sound like much. This girl Sharon
had seemed so nice. Then she turned into a
pain. Was that the whole story? It certainly
didn't explain the deep sense of unease Mack
had been feeling all week.

"Just start anywhere," Aidan coaxed.

"Lilicat and I made a new friend."

Aidan's eyebrows arched. "Female, I hope."

"Of course."

Aidan's face relaxed into a smile. "Well then,
that's great."

"That's what I thought. But . . ."

"But?"

"But here comes the waitress with your banana splits," Dottie said, setting two heaping dishes of ice cream down in front of them. They waited until Dottie had left. Then Aidan raised a long spoon and clinked it against McKenzie's. "Cheers."

"Cheers," Sharon said. She seemed to have appeared out of nowhere.

McKenzie nearly choked on a piece of banana. Suddenly she couldn't breathe, and a numbness spread through her arms and legs. The very sound of Sharon's voice made her feel trapped and scared.

"Hope I'm not interrupting anything," Sharon went on. "But I was wandering around the mall alone and saw you guys sitting here and I thought it would be so great to meet Aidan. Scoot over," she said, giving Aidan a shy smile as she sat down next to him. "I've heard so much about you."

He tried to move over, but the booth was narrow. Sharon was sitting right next to him— practically on top of him, McKenzie thought to herself.

"Uh, Aidan," McKenzie said, trying to keep her cool. "This is Sharon, the new friend I was telling you about. Sharon, this is Aidan." Now that the introductions were over, she added,

"Listen, Sharon, Aidan and I have a lot to talk about—"

McKenzie kept her gaze focused on Sharon, waiting for her to get the message. Sharon just smiled back, as if she hadn't heard.

"We'll definitely see you in school tomorrow," McKenzie said, more pointedly. She said the word *tomorrow* a little louder than she'd meant to.

Sharon's expression didn't change, but her pale cheeks flamed red. Her blue eyes moistened with quick tears as she hurriedly got to her feet.

"I just wanted to meet Aidan," she stammered. "I wasn't going to stay."

"I know, Sharon. It's just that we haven't seen each other for two weeks. . . ."

But Sharon was already running out of the shop.

"Great," McKenzie muttered. "I've done it again."

"What's going on?" Aidan asked.

"Do you think I should go after her?"

Aidan peered out the window. "She's getting into her car."

McKenzie sighed.

"Is this what you wanted to tell me about?" he asked.

McKenzie nodded.

"Well, now seems like a good time."

So McKenzie told him the whole story—the endless phone calls, the fast friendship, the school bus, the fire drill.

"I feel terrible," she finished. "I'd like to help her if I could, but it seems like she wants too much. And to tell you the truth, I'm a little afraid of her. The reason I was lying on the floor in your room was that I had this, like, anxiety attack or something. And when Sharon came in just now I started to feel it all over again. She wants so much from me. It gets my stomach all tied up in knots."

Aidan ran a hand through his already tousled hair. "Look, you can't be totally responsible for her. It sounds like this girl has real problems. Maybe you should try to talk her into seeing the school psychologist. Dr. Karl's a pretty nice guy."

"That's a great idea," McKenzie agreed. She toyed with the melting strawberry ice cream and chocolate syrup on her plate, but it didn't look very appetizing. "I'll call her tonight," she decided.

"Good."

Just making the decision made McKenzie feel a little better.

*   *   *

Dinner made her feel a lot better, especially when they decided to split another dessert—her favorite, pecan pie. The movie was a Chevy Chase comedy that was silly enough to knock all serious thought out of McKenzie's head.

Afterward, she dropped Aidan off at his house, then drove home, humming out loud.

McKenzie turned off the porch light and locked the front door. Her dad had left a granola bar for her on the kitchen table. She was stuffed, but she slipped it into her pocket so he'd think she ate it.

McKenzie stopped short just outside her room. A strip of light was shining under the door. She was sure she'd turned the lights off before she left.

If Jimmy's touching my things, Mack thought, I'll kill him.

She threw open the door, fully prepared to give him a piece of her mind. But she was so surprised by what she saw there that she couldn't speak.

Jimmy was nowhere in sight. Sharon was sitting there, in McKenzie's room, on McKenzie's bed. And she was reading McKenzie's diary.

chapter 6

"Give me that!" McKenzie cried. "How dare you read my diary? What are you doing in my room!"

McKenzie's eyes flicked to her desk—the top drawer was open. She had forgotten to put her diary back in the secret hiding place!

Sharon was gazing back at Mack. She smiled slowly, eerily. The tiny smile broadened. "I knew it," she said softly. "You *can* help me."

"I don't know what you're talking about," said McKenzie. She grabbed the diary from Sharon. "Just go home, and stay away from me and my things, all right? You have no right to be here." She was so angry she was shaking.

"Your little brother said I could wait for you."

"Not in my room, he didn't. Jimmy knows better than that."

"Listen, Mack, you've got to help me," Sharon said pleadingly. "You're the only one who can."

McKenzie stared at her in amazement. "Sharon, you don't listen, do you? I just told you to get out of here." She was sounding like her parents or something, but she was too upset to care.

Sharon shook her head ever so slightly. "I'm not going, Mack. I can't. Mack, I need you!"

McKenzie felt a trickle of sweat run down her back as Sharon stared intensely into her eyes. How much of the diary had Sharon read? Had she seen any of the parts about the visions?

"Sharon, what do you mean, *you need me?*" she asked slowly. But she had a terrible feeling she knew exactly what Sharon meant.

"There's something I have to find out—something very important. . . ."

"Cut it out, Sharon." McKenzie tried to sound calm. "What makes you think *I* have any answers?"

"I had a hunch about you," Sharon said in a tiny voice, barely above a whisper. "That very first night we met—when our hands touched. The way you reacted. You *felt* something."

"Yeah, I got a chill," said McKenzie, trying to sound casual.

"It was more than that," Sharon insisted.

"You knew things about me. You knew I played hockey. You knew Buttons's name. I wasn't sure what it all meant . . . not until tonight. But now I know. You've just got to help me."

McKenzie felt the blood rush to her face. Sharon must have read *a lot* of the diary.

"C'mon, Mack," Sharon said. "You don't have to pretend with me."

"I still don't know what you're talking about."

"Sure you do," Sharon said. "In fact, I'll bet you can read my mind."

chapter 7

"*Read your mind?* You're crazy, Sharon," McKenzie said.

Sharon shook her head. "The diary, Mack: 'I had a vision last night,' " she quoted. " 'And unfortunately, it came true. The girl I saw in my vision—at the amusement park—she really was drowning.' Now who's crazy?"

"You had no right," McKenzie said, her voice breaking.

"Don't worry," Sharon said softly. "I know you're psychic. But your secret's safe with me. I'm your friend, remember? Please, Mack, I'm begging you. You've got to help me!"

"Help you with *what?*" McKenzie asked. Again the feeling of being trapped was overwhelming.

Sharon was standing by the bed now. She moved to the window and stared out into the darkness, as if the answer lay somewhere in the night sky. When she turned back, her face looked pained. "I don't like to talk about it," she said finally.

McKenzie sighed. "Sharon—"

"I know I have to, but I don't like to. It's about . . . Brad." Her voice broke on his name. McKenzie remembered the last time Sharon had tried to broach this subject. Mack hadn't had time, and Sharon had talked to Lilicat instead. Maybe if Sharon would talk about it now, McKenzie thought, she could find some way to get Sharon the kind of help she really needed.

"Okay," McKenzie said. She closed the door to her room. "Let's talk." She pulled up her desk chair. Sharon sat on the edge of the bed, gazing forlornly down at her cowboy boots. Suddenly Blue jumped up on the bed, startling her.

"Sorry," Mack said, but Sharon was petting the cat in long, even strokes.

"That's okay, I love cats," she said, smiling as Blue sniffed her hand.

"You were talking about Brad," McKenzie reminded her, trying to keep her voice soft and soothing.

"Yeah." Sharon caressed the cat in silence for a moment. When she looked up, her eyes were shimmering with tears. "There's more to the story than what I told Lilicat."

Sharon looked at McKenzie for some response.

"Go on," Mack said.

"But if I tell you . . . you've got to swear, and I mean *totally* swear, not to tell anyone. Not a soul. And that means Lilicat, too. Deal?"

Keeping secrets from Lilicat didn't appeal to Mack, but she nodded. "Deal."

"Okay." Sharon let out a deep breath. "I told Lilicat that Brad died in a car accident." Sharon wrung her long, narrow hands. "That's sort of true. But Brad wasn't in a car at the time. We were walking back from a date one night. I remember we had just been to a dance concert at his college, and I was so happy I was pirouetting down the street, and Brad—"

Her voice broke. She put her hands over her face for a moment. When she pulled them away, her cheeks were wet with tears, her eyes red. She went on, "Brad was pretending to lift me, you know, like a dancer. And I guess neither of us was paying much attention, because the street was deserted.

"Then, suddenly, this black Mercedes came

at us out of nowhere." Sharon zoomed her hand angrily through the air. "I mean, it was speeding like crazy. We both saw it. But—"

"Oh, no," McKenzie gasped.

"B-Brad—" Again Sharon stumbled on the name. "He pushed me out of the way, McKenzie. He saved my life."

Now Sharon was sobbing out loud—great heart-wrenching sobs. McKenzie moved closer to her.

"But he couldn't . . . save himself. The car hit him and killed him. And Mack? That car never stopped. Never even slowed down! It just came out of the darkness and vanished into the night."

"Hit-and-run," whispered McKenzie. "How horrible."

Sharon wiped away tears. "The driver was never caught." She slammed her fist into the mattress. Blue jumped down off the bed and landed with a dull thud. "Sorry, Blue," Sharon mumbled, crying freely now.

"Oh, Sharon," McKenzie said. "I'm so sorry."

And she was, sorry for Sharon, sorry she hadn't been able to understand why Sharon was so filled with sadness and need. If only she had known. But she *had* known. She'd felt Sharon's pain the first time she'd touched her. Suddenly McKenzie felt close to tears herself.

"The ring, his class ring," Sharon cried. "Don't you see?" She turned her face to glance up at McKenzie. "All that night, he kept saying this was going to be a really special night. He was going to ask me to go steady . . . to see only him."

A fresh wave of sobs ripped through her and she bent over, rocking with the pain. Looking down at Sharon, she looked small, fragile. Mack wanted to hug her, but something held her back. Fear. "It's okay," Mack mumbled helplessly.

Sharon stood quickly. "No it isn't. It will never be okay unless you help me."

"Sharon." McKenzie stood also, reaching out toward her.

"I want you to use your psychic powers—"

"Oh, Sharon!"

"You know you can do it. I want you to find the driver of that car."

"Sharon," McKenzie began again. "It doesn't work that way. My—" She didn't want to use the word *powers*—"whatever it is, it doesn't work that way. I'm not even sure—"

"You know you can do it," Sharon cut her off bitterly.

"No, that's just it," McKenzie protested. "I *don't* know. It's not something I can turn on and off like a light switch. Yeah, visions sometimes strike me; but I have absolutely no control over when and where. I wish I did, believe me. It can be pretty weird and scary."

Sharon was staring at McKenzie, her face hard.

"I'll tell you what I *will* do," Mack said. "I have a contact at the police station. I'll call up Officer Rizzuto and ask her if the police could look into this case."

"Oh, the police," said Sharon scornfully. "Don't waste your breath. The police gave up long ago."

"Then I probably can't help either," said McKenzie apologetically.

Sharon wiped her eyes with the back of her hand. "You just don't care," she said, sniffling. "You or anybody else."

"That's not true," McKenzie insisted. "You know what I really think? I think it's time to let go. I don't want to get all psychological on you, but dwelling on Brad's accident may be one way of trying to hold on to him."

She paused, wondering if she dared say more. "I mean, even if you could find the driver, that wouldn't bring Brad back to you, would it?"

To her relief, Sharon mumbled, "You're right." But then she added, "The problem is, knowing Brad's killer is off somewhere—free, enjoying his life—makes it impossible to let go of Brad. Can't you understand that?"

McKenzie nodded slowly. She *could* understand that. "Sharon, the truth is, I just don't see how I can do anything about this. I usually need—"

"Some kind of psychic link," Sharon finished her sentence for her. "I know. I've been reading up on this stuff." She jammed her hand into the front pocket of her tight jeans and fished out a crumpled photograph.

"Sharon, I told you, I—"

"Please." Sharon pressed the photo into McKenzie's hand. McKenzie stared down at a snapshot of Sharon and Brad standing arm in arm, gazing into each other's eyes and smiling broadly.

Brad was tall and striking, with dark hair and darker eyes. But it was Sharon who held Mack's gaze. She couldn't believe how happy Sharon looked. The image tugged at her heart. She sighed, yielding. "You won't take no for an answer, will you?" she asked with a smile.

"No," said Sharon, trying to smile back.

"Okay," McKenzie said. "I still don't think this will work, but I'll give it a try."

Sharon rushed forward, reaching out her long, thin arms to give Mack a hug.

"On one condition," Mack added, holding up a hand to stop her.

Sharon looked at her, waiting. She looked as if she would agree to anything.

"Have you met Dr. Karl, the school psychologist?"

Sharon's expression hardened. "I don't need any—"

"Otherwise it's no deal," insisted McKenzie. "Look, you've been through something really rough and you're handling it amazingly well. I can't imagine what I'd do if something that bad happened to me. But everyone thinks Dr. Karl's great. He's there to help. A shoulder to cry on, you know?"

Sharon mouthed an okay.

"Good. I'll go with you tomorrow to set up an appointment." McKenzie put out her hand to shake on it, but again Sharon held out her long thin arms for a hug.

McKenzie felt a moment's panic.

But she smiled and let Sharon hug her.

"I don't know what I'd do without you," Sharon whispered. "I really don't."

"It's okay," Mack mumbled, patting Sharon's back. "I haven't done anything yet."

But Sharon clung to her, whispering, "Thank you, thank you," over and over again.

McKenzie tensed, waiting for the waves of fear, pain.

Nothing came.

So why was there a voice in her head telling her to get away?

chapter 8

Late that night, McKenzie closed her door tightly, lay down on the bed, and studied the photograph Sharon had left her.

It was just an ordinary snapshot of a cute guy. More than cute—Brad was actually quite handsome, with his etched jawline, dark eyes, and dark hair that was longish in front and fell into his eyes in an appealing way. She was glad to have the picture of Brad, so she knew who Sharon was talking about, but what could she possibly see in this?

"Some psychic," McKenzie teased herself aloud.

She stared intently at the photograph clutched

in her hand. The truth was, she had no idea how to begin. She felt extremely foolish. She also felt bad for Sharon. But most of all she felt the girl needed some serious psychological help.

McKenzie forced herself to stop thinking about Sharon. She had to get some sleep or she'd be a total wreck in the morning. She closed her eyes and conjured up Aidan's smiling face. A dreamy warmth flooded through her.

"Good night," she said softly.

From McKenzie's night table, the photo of Sharon and Brad stared down at her as she drifted off toward sleep.

Screams. Shrieks.

But not screams of terror.

A face flashes by, mouth open wide. Another face. And another. The faces are lit up with excitement.

It's a carnival ride. A bunch of high school kids sit locked into tiny green cars, two by two. The cars whip around and around. The kids' hair flies backward in the wind. Mouths gape.

At last the cars slow to a halt. A tattooed man hops over the gate. He lifts the iron bar in each car and lets the passengers escape. They file down the wooden plank. One of the teens is a tall girl with blond hair. She's arm in arm with a dark-haired teenage boy. Sharon and Brad!

Sharon smiles up at Brad. She thanks him for the ride. She is happy. He smiles back. He is happy too.

The moment freezes.

It's a familiar pose. Just like Sharon's snapshot.

Suddenly the background begins to fade and turn white. First the trees, then the people in the distance. Finally, Brad himself begins to disappear. His feet, his legs, his hands, his head. Now he is gone. Sharon is alone. All alone against the vast whiteness, a whiteness so bright it hurts the eyes.

As if shielding herself from the glare, Sharon covers her eyes with her hands.

Then she pulls her hands down. She is crying. The tears flow freely from those pale blue eyes. Iridescent tears stream down her cheeks. Her body jerks with pain. A cry catches in her throat.

The whiteness is darkening now. Darkness closes in around the girl like a threat. Sharon sobs. Hysterically. Uncontrollably. With a pain so deep it cannot be contained.

And then the darkness begins to swallow her up.

McKenzie cried out in the dark. She lurched to a sitting position, suddenly wide awake and alert to danger.

There wasn't a sound in the room. Bewildered, she gazed at her bedside clock. Three a.m. The middle of the night. She was breathing hard. It took a moment for reality to sink in. Nothing terrible had happened. She had dreamed that Brad and Sharon were on a date. But why was Sharon crying like that?

The answer was obvious. Brad is dead, erased from her life.

McKenzie lay back on the pillow and sighed. She thought about Aidan. Losing him would be unbearable. If she were Sharon, she thought, she would never get over it. Never.

"Blue! No!"

McKenzie's cat was rubbing his ear hard against the kitchen doorway as McKenzie got ready for school on Friday morning.

"He seems to be getting worse, not better," Mrs. Gold commented, pouring herself a cup of coffee. McKenzie had to agree.

So did the vet, whom McKenzie visited before she went to school. "It looks like he's been rubbing the ear and irritating it," Dr. Grumbach said. Reading the worry in McKenzie's eyes, he added kindly, "Don't worry. Blue will be fine. But I'm afraid he's going to have to spend the night with us."

Sometimes Blue seemed to understand English. Right then he looked up at McKenzie and opened his mouth in a silent meow.

McKenzie gave him a quick kiss and hurried off. With any luck she'd only miss a few minutes of her first-period class.

"You weren't on the bus. I was worried about you," a soft voice called when McKenzie came out of Miss Peters's homeroom twenty minutes later. Sharon was waiting by the door.

"Let's go," McKenzie said. "It's time to make that appointment we talked about."

She was careful not to say Dr. Karl's name, in case other students were listening.

"Oh, I really don't think—"

"We made a deal, remember?" McKenzie said. "Come on."

But the secretary in Dr. Karl's office told them that the counselor was out for the day. "I can give you an appointment for Monday," the secretary said, checking the date book. McKenzie elbowed Sharon. "Okay, Monday," Sharon agreed.

"Well, I kept my part of the deal," she said as they left the office. "Now, what did you find out?"

McKenzie hadn't been sure she should tell

Sharon about her dream. But now that she was standing beside her, now that Sharon was staring at her with those sorrowful blue eyes, it seemed wrong to withhold any information. "I had a dream about you and Brad last night," McKenzie began.

Sharon's eyes were large to begin with, but they got even wider as McKenzie recounted the dream. "That's incredible," she said. "You just described our first date. We went to the McCloskie Street Fair and Carnival. Do you have the photo with you?"

McKenzie fished it out of her knapsack. "Look!" Sharon said triumphantly, pointing a long, thin finger at a curve in the background. "You can just make out the edge of the Ferris wheel. See? My friend Gina was there, and she snapped this picture of us." She offered the photo back to McKenzie.

"I don't think I can get any more out of it," McKenzie said.

Sharon looked disappointed. "Why not? You already had a vision. That proves I was right. You *can* help me."

"I'm not so sure," McKenzie said.

"Let's just try," Sharon said. "That's all I'm asking. Let's—"

The bell rang shrilly and McKenzie said, "I gotta run." It was a relief to escape from Sharon into the crowded hallway.

For the rest of the day, McKenzie managed to avoid bumping into Sharon. After school she holed up in the *Guardian* office, transcribing notes from her mini-tape recorder for her next column. She was almost done with the honor code piece. The copy was due on Monday. But she had the office all to herself and the work was going quickly.

At least, she thought she had the office to herself.

Then she looked up.

Sharon was standing right over her. McKenzie gasped.

"Sorry," Sharon said, flushing. "I didn't mean to scare you."

"Well, you did. I didn't hear you come in."

"I'm wearing sneakers today," Sharon said, looking down at her feet. "Not those clunky cowboy boots."

McKenzie held one hand against her chest. "Okay, I think I can breathe again."

"Good." Sharon gestured at a cluttered desk in the corner. "Carol Ann says my first job is to take on this filing. Yuck!"

"Well," McKenzie said, "it has been piling

up." Though what she wanted to say was, "Forget it, go home, do it some other time. And *leave me alone.*"

But Sharon was clearly not about to leave—or start filing. "I have a few things of Brad's I want to show you," she said, holding a gray envelope out to McKenzie. "Maybe it will help you to see more of what happened."

"Oh, I can't right now," McKenzie protested. "I've got an important deadline coming up."

Sharon stared at her blankly for a moment. Then her eyes flashed with anger. She raised her voice. "Forget your deadline. *This* is important. I need your help—right now." She practically screamed the last words.

McKenzie flinched and pushed her chair backward. She looked at Sharon nervously, not sure what to do or say next. The blond girl seemed almost out of control.

But Sharon's anger disappeared as quickly as it had come. "I'm sorry," she said in her normal soft voice. "It's just that this whole business has been driving me crazy."

For a minute, McKenzie thought that Sharon really *was* crazy. But, as usual, she still couldn't help feeling sorry for her. "Okay," Mack said. "Let's see what you've got."

She was afraid Sharon was going to cry again

or something. But the blond girl quickly composed herself. "Thank you," she said. "I won't take up much of your time, I promise. This," Sharon said, waving the envelope over McKenzie's desk, "is all I have left of Brad."

She tilted the envelope and poured out a chocolate heart wrapped in red foil, a folded note, and a thick gold band with a green stone in the center.

McKenzie turned Brad's class ring over in her fingers.

"That's the ring he had with him, the night he—" Sharon broke off.

McKenzie slipped the ring onto the fourth finger of her left hand, trying to picture Sharon and Brad together. But she felt nothing.

McKenzie took off the ring and picked up the chocolate, throwing Sharon a questioning glance.

"Just some candy he gave me once. He liked to give me a little present every day, as a surprise."

"Every day?"

Sharon nodded. "Nothing major. It was almost always something to eat. I don't know why I saved this."

McKenzie reached for the note and began reading it to herself.

Dear Blue Eyes,

I know we just went out last night, Shari, but I was wondering if you might want to go out again tonight? And how about tomorrow night? Are you free then? And what about the day after tomorrow?

Love,
Brad

"He wasn't much of a writer," Sharon said, peering over McKenzie's shoulder. "This is the only letter he ever wrote me, the whole six months we were dating."

The paper was mottled with tear stains. *This has been read and reread many times since the accident,* McKenzie thought as she carefully re-folded the note. "Sorry, Sharon," she said. "I'm still not getting anything. I warned you, I've never been able to control—"

"Give me your hands," Sharon ordered.

"Huh?"

"You don't just see things, do you? You *feel* them! That night we first met. When your hand touched mine, you felt something, didn't you? Didn't you?"

"Yes," McKenzie admitted. "I felt a lot of pain."

"All the pain that the driver of that car caused

me," Sharon cried, her eyes burning. "Now give me your hands."

Feeling a little embarrassed, McKenzie glanced toward the office door.

"No one's coming," Sharon promised.

McKenzie held out her hands, and Sharon grasped them tightly. Her blue eyes locked on to Mack's.

"Tell me what you feel," Sharon whispered. "Tell me what you see."

"I—"

"You've got to tell me what happened to him."

"You're hurting me!"

"What do you see?!"

McKenzie suddenly felt a strong urge to break eye contact. She closed her eyes and felt a violent current surge through her body. She let out a gasp.

"What is it?" demanded Sharon, squeezing McKenzie's hands even tighter. "What do you see?"

McKenzie gripped back. A blur of images were flying through her brain. She could barely breathe.

"I see Brad," she whispered.

Sharon squeezed even harder. Both girls' hands were trembling.

"He's alone," Mack went on. "Walking."

"Walking where?"

The image was hazy. Suddenly it widened. "A road. A dirt road. There's a cottage in the distance."

"A country road?"

"Yes."

McKenzie opened her eyes. Sharon was breathing hard. *"What?"* Sharon demanded. "Why are you stopping?"

"It went away," McKenzie said simply. She flexed her hands, trying to get the blood flowing again.

"Sorry," Sharon apologized. "I guess I squeezed a little hard." There was a wild look in her eyes.

"Did that mean anything to you?" McKenzie asked, massaging her temples. Her head was throbbing.

"No," Sharon said. "Brad lived on campus, in a dorm. Where is this cottage? Can you see him? When is this happening?"

"I can't see anything now," McKenzie said. "But it seemed very far away."

"Far away?"

"I don't know. I told you, Sharon, I don't have control over this stuff. I can't just pull out the information I need like from some encyclopedia."

"Isn't there some way you can get more details?"

McKenzie shrugged. "It's very iffy, but sometimes . . . well, there have been times when I've gone into a room where someone has just been and I've gotten a strong sense of that person and been able to kind of follow him. But here I have no connection. I mean, Brad's dead. . . ."

"Wait," said Sharon. "I've got it. Why don't I take you to his dorm? That was the last place he lived. Maybe you'd sense something there!"

"Maybe," said Mack doubtfully.

"Let's go right now."

McKenzie looked at Sharon with dismay. "I can't," she said. "I've got work to do, remember? I shouldn't have even taken this much time."

"Mack, we've got to go *now!*" Sharon cried, striding impatiently around the room. "Please! If you don't go with me, I'll go crazy! I—I'll kill myself!"

McKenzie saw a quick image of Sharon standing in the path of the school bus. "I've got to know who did it, can't you see that?" Sharon insisted.

"I *can* see that," McKenzie said slowly. Anything to calm Sharon down.

"So," Sharon said, "yes or no?"

Mack was about to say no, but Sharon didn't give her a chance. "Mack, I'm begging you." Her voice quavered. "I've got no one else to turn to. You don't know what it's like. It's like walking around with a knife in your heart. I can't stand it!"

"Okay," McKenzie said finally. "I'll try it." She reached for her tape recorder and dropped it into her knapsack. "But I still don't think this is going to work."

Suddenly joyful, Sharon whooped. "Oh, thank you, Mack. I knew you wouldn't let me down. And don't worry—it *will* work. It *has* to!"

"I hope so," McKenzie said. She popped her disk out of the computer. She could finish the column at home, she figured, and bring it back on Monday. She tried to smile. "Let's go."

"We'll take my car. I brought it today," Sharon said.

The parking lot was deserted when McKenzie got into the passenger seat and watched Sharon start the car. Sharon's hand was trembling. Her key chain—which was loaded with everything from a silver mirror to a troll doll with belly-length orange hair—dangled and jangled from the ignition as she peeled out of the lot.

McKenzie snapped on her shoulder safety belt. Sharon was soon driving over the limit. "He went to Cadaret College?" Mack asked as they sped toward the campus.

Sharon nodded.

"How did you meet him?" McKenzie asked.

"It's kind of a funny story," Sharon began. "He and some of his friends from college had jobs as lifeguards at the community pool my parents belonged to. The minute I saw him, I knew he was for me. It wasn't only that he was so gorgeous. There was just something between us.

"Anyway, he hardly paid any attention to me—until one day I decided I had to get his attention. So I climbed to the top of this real high diving board and jumped into the pool. The thing is, I'm a pretty lousy swimmer and I kind of panicked underwater. By the time I came up I was really scared and Brad had to dive in and rescue me. After that day, he knew I was alive, and eventually he asked me out."

McKenzie listened to Sharon's story uneasily. She had no trouble picturing Sharon so desperate to get Brad's attention that she jumped off the high board—not knowing and not caring whether she could handle the deep water or not.

"Sharon," McKenzie said after a bit, "I really don't think we're going to be able to track down the driver who hit Brad."

"I can't afford to think that way," Sharon said grimly. "You'll help me. You'll see."

Sharon parked on a tree-lined street outside a quad of dorms. She moved quickly across the lawn, staring straight ahead at one of the large, modern brick buildings. A chill wind ruffled her green parka, whipped her straight blond hair. Watching the slight figure staring so intently at the dorm, McKenzie felt another ache of pity. Sharon looked so forlorn.

"That was his room." Sharon pointed as McKenzie came up beside her. "Second floor, third from the left."

McKenzie counted, found it, and stared at the curtainless window. It looked dark, dead.

"And this," Sharon said with a sweep of her delicate hand, "is the street where it happened."

McKenzie followed the gesture. The street was wide and deserted, just as Sharon had described. Across the street were an all-night pizza place, a Store 24, and a by-the-pound laundry.

McKenzie walked out into the middle of the road. "I hate to do this to you, Sharon," she said. "But can you remember where you were standing?"

Sharon bit her lip as she looked around. "Over there," she said.

McKenzie moved to the right. "Here?"

"Even more in the center."

McKenzie took another step. "Here?"

Sharon nodded.

"And you were dancing, right?"

Sharon nodded more slowly. "Don't make me do that," she begged.

McKenzie reached out and touched her arm. "It's okay. Then you turned and saw the car, right?"

They both turned and looked up the street.

A car was coming toward them.

But it wasn't black, and it wasn't speeding. There was plenty of time for McKenzie and Sharon to get out of the way.

"Nothing," McKenzie said as they stepped up onto the curb. "I'm getting nothing, no signal, no—"

McKenzie stopped short in the middle of the sidewalk. She suddenly had the eerie feeling that there *was* something—something large and horrible—and it was looming right behind her back.

"What is it?" Sharon asked her. "What's wrong?"

Mack felt her mouth fall slack.

"Mack?" Sharon said.

She didn't answer. Instead, she turned around slowly. Then she froze again.

The street was gone.

Brad is standing in a long line. A movie line. He's with Sharon. Sharon is laughing. Or is it Sharon? No, it's not, it's some other girl with long hair. A redhead. Lots of lipstick. Brad is saying something to the girl. She touches his arm. She takes off her sunglasses. Green eye shadow. Everything seems to be fine. The line moves forward. Brad and the girl approach the ticket window. Brad buys tickets. They're the last ones to get in. The people right after them are sent away.

The marquee is visible now. The movie they're going to see is Esmeralda.

"*Esmeralda?*" McKenzie murmured.

"Mack! What is it? What's wrong?"

McKenzie blinked her eyes rapidly. She was standing on the side of the road again. The street, the cars, the stores—everything was back where it belonged. Sharon had her by the arm.

McKenzie rubbed her face hard with both hands, trying to clear her head.

Then it hit her. *Esmeralda!*

The realization struck her with the force of a blow. She couldn't keep the shock from registering on her face.

"*What?*" Sharon demanded.

"Oh my God," McKenzie mumbled, amazed. A look of joy began to replace the confusion on her face.

Sharon started to shake her. "Tell me!"

"You—you're not going to believe this!" Mack said, stammering with confusion. "I can hardly believe it myself . . . but Brad is alive!"

chapter 9

Two splotches appeared on Sharon's pale cheeks. "What are you talking about, McKenzie? Is this some kind of terrible joke?"

"I saw him," said McKenzie. "I saw him standing in line with a girl. He was going to see a movie—*Esmeralda.*"

"So?"

"So that movie just opened! Brad is alive. I know it!"

"That's ridiculous," Sharon said. "I was there when he died."

"Well, all I know is what I just saw," McKenzie said firmly.

Sharon looked dumbfounded. "You said he was with a girl?" she said shrilly. "What girl?"

"I don't know," said McKenzie. "Just some girl. . . ."

"Why are you saying these things?" Sharon cried. "What are you trying to do to me?"

"I didn't mean to upset you," McKenzie said softly. "I thought you'd be happy. Don't you get it? There must have been some kind of mistake."

Sharon spun around, facing the dorm, Brad's old window. When she turned back, her face was even redder. "If he's alive," she said with great intensity, "then where is he? Where is my boyfriend, Mack? Can I call him up? Can I hold him in my arms?"

"I have no idea where he is," McKenzie admitted. "But I'm telling you, he's out there somewhere."

"If you know he's alive, then you must know where he is," Sharon insisted. She pointed an accusing finger, holding it close to McKenzie's face. "You're not telling me the truth! Tell me where he is!"

"I don't know! I swear!"

Sharon looked as if she were about to say something—something awful, Mack thought, judging by the look on her face. But she kept her mouth clamped shut as she turned and started back toward her car, kicking a discarded Pepsi can out of the way. The can skidded across the street, spinning slowly to a halt.

Sharon got behind the wheel and McKenzie slipped into the passenger seat. Neither girl said a word; they both looked straight ahead.

Then Sharon pulled out. She's worried about something, McKenzie suddenly sensed. Very worried. But about what? That my vision will prove to be just another dead end, another false hope? That I'm wrong about Brad being alive?

She settled back into the seat and tried to put the whole business out of her mind. Sharon was driving fast, which suited McKenzie just fine. Being with Sharon was exhausting. And besides, she still had her column to do—*and* her parents would start to worry if she wasn't home soon.

McKenzie didn't realize just how much she was looking forward to leaving Sharon until she saw her house, the porch light already on. Her spirits lifted immediately.

Then the house flew by.

"Hey!" McKenzie said. "Stop the car."

Sharon continued to stare straight ahead as she swerved onto Oak Lawn.

"What are you doing?" McKenzie demanded.

"You're not going home until you tell me where my boyfriend is," Sharon said.

"What are you talking about? I already told you everything I know."

Sharon didn't respond.

"Sharon, I promise you. I'm doing the best I can."

Sharon parked the car at the end of the Oak Lawn cul-de-sac. The porch light at the Roderick house was not on.

"Fine," Mack said. "Be that way. I'll walk home." She started to get out of the car, but Sharon reached out and put a restraining hand on her arm.

"I'm sorry," Sharon said matter-of-factly. "But that just isn't acceptable."

"Huh? What isn't?"

"You going home."

"Are you out of your mind?" McKenzie pulled her arm free. "I'll go home whenever I feel like it. Who do you think you are?"

Sharon just smiled. "The question is—who do you think *you* are? If you leave now, I'll tell the whole school you're this crazy person who's got psychic powers!"

chapter 10

"You've got to be kidding," McKenzie said.

Sharon didn't answer, but the expression on her face said it all: She was dead serious.

"You're threatening me?"

Sharon shrugged. "I need to find Brad."

"I thought we were friends," said McKenzie.

"I thought so too."

Furious and frustrated, McKenzie slammed out of the car and headed for the house. "I'll try for ten minutes," she called back angrily over her shoulder. "Then I'm out of here."

Sharon fumbled through the many gadgets on her key chain until she found the front-door key. McKenzie could hear Buttons yipping at the door. "Buttons, hush!" Sharon called, hurrying to open the lock. "We're going to have to be quiet," she told McKenzie in a soft voice. "My mother always takes a nap before dinner."

The entry hall was dark. Buttons jumped up, wild to be petted. Sharon ignored her as she flicked on a light. "I'll feed you later," she told the dog sharply. Then, to McKenzie, she said, "This way," and glided up the long, wide stairs. McKenzie followed. Buttons stayed downstairs, watching the girls and whining pitifully.

Sharon walked down a long hallway toward the back of the house, past a bedroom, past a small bathroom, until they came to a closed door. She opened the door, and motioned McKenzie to go first. "Our guest room," she said, turning on the overhead light.

The room looked like a prison cell. Bare white walls. An unmade bed. One high, narrow window that looked out onto darkness.

"We haven't really got it fixed up yet," said Sharon with a strange giggle.

"Look," McKenzie said. "I'm not in the mood for joking around. You've got me here. Now what do you want me to do?"

Sharon clucked her tongue. "Don't be impatient with me, McKenzie Gold. I don't like it when you're impatient."

McKenzie sighed.

Sharon went on, "Now *I'm* being patient with *you*—"

"Patient. Right!"

Sharon eyed her levelly for a long, silent moment. "Okay," she said. "If that's the way you want to be, let's get on with it."

"Get on with what?"

"Just tell me where Brad is."

"I already told you a hundred times: I don't know. I can't just order up a vision like a pizza."

"Then how come you're so sure he's alive?" Sharon turned and asked.

"I told you, the movie—"

"That's not good enough, Mack. I want you to prove to me that he's alive."

"How can I do that when—"

"Tell me where he is right now. Right NOW!"

At that moment, Sharon gave McKenzie a look that made her shudder. She felt as if a cold and clammy pair of hands were about to close around her neck.

"I'm leaving now," McKenzie said, starting for the door.

Sharon blocked her way. "You haven't answered my question. Where is Brad?"

"I don't know!"

"Well, try!"

McKenzie closed her eyes. If only she could

see where he was. Then this whole crazy episode
would end. But her mind was dark and blank.
All she could feel was a dull pain throbbing in
her forehead. She opened her eyes again. Sharon's angry face reappeared before her like something in a nightmare.

"I can't see a thing," McKenzie told her.
Sharon moved closer. "Look, I've had it," Mack
said angrily. "You can tell the whole school I'm
a witch, for all I care. Just don't ever speak to
me again."

Sharon stared down at the floor, dejected,
depressed. All the fight seemed to have gone
out of her. I refuse to fall for that self-pity act,
McKenzie told herself. She started toward the
door.

And then the blow came.

Sharon sprang into action, throwing the weight
of her whole body against McKenzie, knocking
her backward to the floor.

McKenzie scrambled to her feet, but Sharon
was already out in the hall.

The door slammed in McKenzie's face.

She recovered quickly from the shock and
reached for the doorknob. But not quickly
enough. There was a menacing little click.

Sharon had locked her in.

chapter 11

"Sharon!" McKenzie called through the closed door.

Out in the hall, she could hear Sharon giggling. The laughter was high-pitched, out of control—crazy.

"Very funny, Sharon. Now let me out."

She waited. There was silence. "Sharon, don't be an idiot. Open the door."

"Tell me where Brad is," came the response.

McKenzie lay her head against the door.

"When you're ready to tell," Sharon said, "you can come out."

"Sharon, if you don't open the door this second, I'm going to scream and wake up your mom."

Sharon laughed out loud. "Then you'll have to scream pretty loud."

McKenzie felt a jolt of panic. "What do you mean?"

"My mom's not home. She's visiting her sister . . . in Tucson."

"Let me out," Mack said quietly. "Please."

She stared at the door. It looked solid, unyielding. It looked as if it would never open again. She waited a moment more. Stay calm, she ordered herself. But her heart was racing.

"Sharon?" she tried again. No answer.

Suddenly, a terrifying thought occurred to McKenzie: Sharon wasn't standing outside the locked door anymore. She was sure of it.

"SHARON!" She pounded on the door several times.

C'mon, McKenzie, get a grip, she coaxed herself. You tell yourself to stay calm, and the next moment you're pounding on the door like a lunatic.

Like a lunatic. Like the lunatic who had her locked in this little cell.

Then she checked the keyhole.

Sharon's blue eye stared back at her.

McKenzie jumped back.

More wild giggling from the hall.

McKenzie walked away from the door in

disgust. Maybe if she ignored her, Sharon would get bored with this game and unlock the door. She looked around the bare room. Before she could make a thorough inspection, Sharon's voice came through the door:

"Listen, McKenzie," Sharon said with infuriating calm. "If he's really alive, where is he? It's that simple. If you tell me, you'll be fine. If you don't, you'll be sorry. Very sorry."

"I'm trying," McKenzie said. "But you've got to let me out of here."

"I don't *have* to do anything," Sharon said. McKenzie could picture a small smile playing across Sharon's thin lips. *"I'm* in control now, get it? Now, you can stay in there for a few minutes, or you can stay in there for a couple of weeks; it's—"

"Weeks?" McKenzie was sure she hadn't heard right.

"Yes, Mack, *weeks*. My mom will be back from Tucson in two weeks, so—"

Now it was McKenzie's turn to laugh. It didn't sound like her own laugh. It sounded hysterical. "Listen, Sharon, my parents are already wondering where I am. If they don't hear from me soon, they're going to come looking for me *tonight*, okay?"

Silence.

Let her think that one over, McKenzie thought.
She waited.

Then, through the closed door, Sharon said,
"I've already thought of that."

The door swung open.

McKenzie's mouth dropped open.

Sharon was standing in the doorway. She was
holding a long, sharp knife.

chapter 12

"Stand back," *Sharon* instructed.

McKenzie did as she was told.

Sharon kicked the door shut behind her and took a quick step toward McKenzie. The knife was now pressed against McKenzie's throat.

"Call," Sharon hissed. Only then did Mack notice the cordless phone clutched in Sharon's left hand.

Sweat began trickling down McKenzie's forehead. A salty drop ran into her eye, but she made no attempt to wipe it away. She swallowed and felt the edge of the knife against her throat. "Call who?"

The knife pressed harder. "Don't be a fool,

Mack. Call your parents. Tell them you're going to spend the weekend with me.''

McKenzie didn't dare move her head. But she could still move her eyes enough to look at Sharon directly. "Sharon—"

"Call."

McKenzie blinked. She stared at the phone, trying to focus on the tiny numbers. What was her number? For a moment, she couldn't remember.

With shaky fingers, she punched in the numbers.

"Hello?" It was her mother's voice, her mother's calm, familiar voice. "Hello?"

"Mom?"

"McKenzie?"

"This is McKenzie," she continued stupidly. Sharon was glaring at her.

"Hi, honey," Mrs. Gold said. "Where are you? I was starting to worry."

Starting to worry? Believe me, McKenzie thought, it's time to go ahead and worry in a big way. "I'm at Sharon's," she said, trying to keep her voice steady.

"Oh. Well, you'd better hurry up. Your father's been home for fifteen minutes now and his stomach is rumbling."

There had to be some way to let her mother

know something was wrong. Some way without tipping Sharon off.

Sharon's blue eyes bored into hers. She couldn't think. "Uh, Mom, that's why I called. Sharon asked me to stay for dinner."

Sharon's grip on the knife tightened visibly, her knuckles going white.

"For the weekend, actually."

"I thought you didn't like her very much," Mrs. Gold said.

McKenzie pressed the phone against her ear, praying Sharon hadn't heard that. As if in response, Sharon pressed her own ear to the phone.

"No, I do," McKenzie said quickly. "Anyway, can I?"

"Well . . ." Mrs. Gold sighed. "I wish you had asked me earlier. I already put the lamb chops in."

McKenzie waited, sweating. Then she had an idea.

"McKenzie? Are you all right?"

"Yeah, of course. I'm just sorry that I'll be missing Dad's tuna casserole Sunday night."

"What?" her mother asked. "The Tuna Casserole of Death? Why wouldn't you want to miss that? Sweetie, you sound funny. You're sure you're fine?"

Sharon pulled her head back, giving Mc-
Kenzie a threatening look.

"Absolutely. I'm totally fine," McKenzie said,
resigned.

"Okay, then," Mrs. Gold said. "Good. Well,
have fun, sweetheart. I've gotta run."

And her mother clicked off.

"She hung up," McKenzie said. She was close
to tears.

Sharon took the phone. "Good." She backed
up to the door and opened it, pointing the knife
at McKenzie the whole time. "When you're
ready to tell me where Brad is, you can go
home."

"What if I can't?"

Sharon just shrugged. Then, "Have a good
night," she said, locking the door again. Her
footsteps echoed down the long hallway.

McKenzie stared at the closed door in amazement. Okay, she told herself. Calm. Calm. Calm.

She said the word over and over, more and
more quickly. Her heart was pounding. She
moved to the door and listened. She couldn't
hear a thing.

McKenzie tried the door. The knob wouldn't
even turn. She studied the room again. It was
small. She tried pounding on one of the walls.

They were thick. Just the one window. High up. She had to stand on tiptoe to look out.

It took a moment to make out what she was seeing. Way down below was an overgrown, weed-filled garden. Lots of trees. Just as she'd thought, she was now in one of the back rooms. There wasn't another house in sight.

The image of her and Lilicat driving here from Pizza Town came back to her.

"Don't you hate living all the way at the end of a dead end like this?" she heard Lilicat ask.

Sharon laughing. *"Way out in the sticks, no neighbors to hang out with? It's a teenage girl's dream!"*

She could open the window and scream, but who would hear her? Who besides Sharon?

Mack pulled the bed over to the window, stood up on it, and peered out. It was a long way down. There was no tree close enough to grab on to. But maybe there was a drainage pipe or something?

She unlocked the window and pushed up.

Nothing happened.

She pushed harder, straining with all her might. The window was jammed shut. She looked around for something to smash the glass with. Then she stopped and looked back at the window again. What was she thinking of? That narrow modern window—there was no way she could climb through it.

She wiped her dusty hands on her jeans and sat down on the bed, her head in her hands.

Okay, she told herself, time for Plan B.

But what *was* Plan B? Wait it out, she decided. Hope Sharon didn't do anything too weird, like deprive her of food or water or use of the bathroom.

Some plan. But it was all she had, all she had to hold on to.

For the first time, she realized how exhausted she was. She was bone tired. She was also drenched in sweat, and there was greasy dirt on her palms and face.

She unlaced her sneakers. Maybe if she lay down, something would occur to her.

Something useful, like Brad's whereabouts.

But all that came to her were more tears. And after that, a deep and dreamless sleep.

McKenzie opened her eyes. She saw blond hair. The top of Sharon's head. Then she felt one of her hands being lifted.

McKenzie's eyes widened in horror as she realized what was happening. Sharon was carefully tying her hands together, trying not to wake her up.

McKenzie kicked out violently, struggling to escape. But she couldn't move her legs.

They were already tied.

chapter 13

"*If you start* screaming," Sharon said calmly, "I'm going to have to gag you. It's your choice."

"Let me go, you crazy—"

"Just use your powers and you're out of here," Sharon said.

McKenzie's breath was coming in gulps. She tried to slow it down, to wake up, to think. "Sharon, I know you're obsessed with getting revenge on the driver who killed Brad, but . . ."

Sharon rammed her face up close to McKenzie's, only inches away. "But what?" she asked. Her lower lip was trembling.

"But . . . but that's no reason to hurt *me*. Or yourself. You're going to get into trouble; you know that, don't you? This is illegal, what you're doing. But if you let me go, I promise I won't tell anyone."

Sharon wasn't listening. She was laughing. Louder and harder than Mack had ever heard her.

"You *promise*," Sharon repeated in a voice full of scorn. Her face contorted with sudden fury. "You make me *sick!*"

She darted forward, and McKenzie shrank back—as far as the ropes that bound her would allow. "Sick, sick, sick," Sharon hissed.

Sharon moved around the room, touching the wall here, there, turning each corner sharply, like a caged animal. The sweet girl that McKenzie had met at Pizza Town just a few weeks ago was gone. Totally gone.

Sharon suddenly turned and headed for the door. "Where are you going?" McKenzie asked desperately. "Sharon, don't leave me here."

"Oh, I won't," Sharon said with a nasty chuckle. "I'll be back, you can count on it. And if you can't tell me where Brad is by the time I come back, then . . ."

Then what? McKenzie didn't even want to imagine.

"Then I will teach you a little lesson," Sharon said, overenunciating the last words.

She was gone. The door locked once more.

As if McKenzie could go anywhere. She swung her bound legs onto the floor. She could hop. But that wouldn't get her very far.

She lay back down. Her hands and feet were beginning to go numb and tingly from the ropes. *Numb and tingly?* Something jogged in her memory. What? She tried to think.

Abruptly, McKenzie began to buck with all her might, straining against the ropes and groaning in frustration. Panic seized her. She felt the walls closing in—felt as if she couldn't breathe.

Then, just as abruptly, she lay still, totally still.

She was picturing herself in Aidan's room.

And in Sharon's room that first night.

So this was why she had felt that strange tingling, why she had felt tied up at Aidan's. The sensation had been a message, about the future.

Her power. That was the only thing left for her now. To use the power. Sharon had made it very clear what she wanted. Now all McKenzie had to do was . . .

She shut her eyes tight. Think!

Brad!

She tried to picture him—the handsome face, the etched jawline she had seen in the snapshot and in her visions. The movie theater. The cottage.

McKenzie reviewed the images as if she were flipping through a photo album. But she couldn't lose her sense of detachment. The images were old. They were dead.

Her power! What a horrible joke. If there was something good about having her gift, at the moment she couldn't see it. Where was the power when she needed it?

She felt so alone, so deserted, that she started to cry again. And because she could barely move, the warm tears leaked down her cheeks and collected in her ears. She didn't even hear the door open again.

Sharon entered, one hand behind her back. "Aw, Mack," she said with what seemed like genuine sympathy. "Don't cry."

"Please let me go," McKenzie begged.

Sharon smiled compassionately. "You know the arrangement."

"But I can't do it." Another sob escaped her.

"Are you sure?" Sharon asked softly, slowly, like someone talking to a child.

McKenzie nodded.

Sharon shrugged. Then she took her hand from behind her back. She was holding a large pair of shears.

"What are you going to do with those?" McKenzie cried.

Sharon reached out with her free hand. McKenzie shrank back, but it was no use. Sharon fingered McKenzie's thick auburn hair. "Beautiful," she murmured. "Beautiful. No wonder Aidan likes you."

Then she grabbed a lock of hair—right in the front—and opened the shears' large silver blades.

"No!" McKenzie cried.

Snip.

The lock of hair fluttered past her eyes. She didn't dare move her head for fear of being blinded.

Sharon looked oddly calm. Then, without warning, she was shouting. "You're not telling me the truth!" She held the shears to another lock of hair. Then, back in her calm voice, she said, "Let's give you a nice set of bangs."

Snip.

"I can't do it!" cried McKenzie. "I'm trying—"

Snip.

"A nice set of bangs just like a little girl."

Snip.

"You've got to tell me something more, Mack." That calm voice.

Snip.

"Stop hiding things from me."

"I'm not! Please believe me," McKenzie pleaded.

Snip.

"What happened to him, McKenzie? Tell me soon or the rest of your hair is history. How would your cute boyfriend like you with a crew cut?"

"STOP!"

Suddenly, Sharon did stop. She smiled. "I almost forgot. I have a surprise for you. Can you guess what it is?"

McKenzie mouthed the word *no*.

"I'll be right back," Sharon said. "And when I come back, you'd better be ready to talk."

She was gone.

Think! McKenzie silently screamed at herself. She stared at the door, rigid with fear but trying desperately to think. She was in real danger now. Could Sharon possibly be capable of murder? Was there any way out of this nightmare?

But the door was already swinging open again.

Sharon stood there with the shears in one hand.

In her other hand she was holding Blue.

chapter 14

*"**What is he** doing here?"* McKenzie asked, horrified.

Sharon grinned. "I did you a favor. I picked him up from the vet's during study hall and brought him back here. I told Dr. Grumbach you couldn't bear to spend the night without him."

Blue gave a plaintive meow. "Sweet little kitty," Sharon said, smiling. "Dr. Grumbach says he's going to be fine, as long as he takes his medicine and gets lots of rest. Oh, and you have to treat him real gentle. Dr. Grumbach made a point of that. Right, Blue?" She gave the old black cat a squeeze. Blue tried to wriggle free, but she held him tightly.

"PUT THAT CAT DOWN!" McKenzie said, fury rising in her throat.

Sharon looked surprised. "What's this? *You're* giving *me* orders?"

Sharon opened and closed the shears. Opened and closed. The sound of the blades sliding against each other was hideous.

"Sharon, he's an old cat, he's sick, and—" McKenzie's voice broke.

"Then why don't you"—Sharon raised the open shears and shrieked—"TELL ME ABOUT THE ACCIDENT! NOW!"

McKenzie shut her eyes. "I'm trying!"

She could hear Sharon breathing hard.

She had to do something—and fast. Sharon wanted a vision? Well, she'd just have to give her one.

"I see the street," McKenzie began suddenly, desperately trying to remember everything Sharon had told her.

"That's more like it," Sharon said.

"You're there—with Brad."

"Go on." Her voice was louder. McKenzie could feel her coming closer.

"You're happy," McKenzie said, forcing herself not to open her eyes.

"Yes." Sharon didn't sound satisfied.

"Very happy."

"Yes."

"You're dancing."

A pause, then, "Dancing?"

"Doing pirouettes."

"Go on," Sharon said in a whisper.

"Yes," McKenzie said, eyes still shut. "Suddenly . . ."

"Suddenly . . .?"

"A car is speeding toward you in the darkness. It's about to hit Brad. It—"

"What kind of car is it?" Sharon broke in.

McKenzie's eyes snapped open. What kind of car? The question echoed in her brain. She knew Sharon had told her, but she couldn't remember. "It's—it's a BMW. A *black* one," she added quickly. "Just like you said."

"Are you sure?"

McKenzie nodded vigorously.

Sharon stared at her, trembling. By the look on her face, McKenzie knew she'd made a terrible mistake. She suddenly felt sick to her stomach. The room began to sway.

Sharon's expression twisted with rage. "No, McKenzie," she said. "It was a black *Mercedes!* You're FAKING IT! I knew it! You just made this whole little *vision* up. You're probably lying about everything. You know who was driving but you won't tell me," she wailed, jabbing the shears at McKenzie.

"I *don't* know," Mack insisted. "I really don't know! Believe me—I'd tell you if I did."

Sharon stared at her for what seemed an eternity.

Then she slowly opened and closed the shears again.

She positioned the shears' sharp point against Blue's furry, fat belly.

McKenzie began to sob.

chapter 15

The telephone rang in a nearby room, and McKenzie choked back her sobs. She and Sharon stared at each other. Finally Sharon dropped Blue to the floor and left to answer it, locking the door behind her. "Blue," McKenzie cried.

The black cat moved fast for his years, hurrying across the room and springing onto the bed. He padded over to McKenzie and licked her face. Then he began meowing pitifully.

"It's okay, Blue," whispered Mack, wishing there were someone around to say the same thing to her. "Shh," she said when he continued to meow.

McKenzie's entire body tensed as she strained

to hear Sharon's phone conversation in the other room.

"Hello?" Sharon was saying. "Lilicat! Hi! How are you?"

She sounded so cheerful! So totally unlike the person who had been torturing McKenzie and Blue just a moment before.

"What? Yeah—but she's in the shower right now. Can she call you back later? Okay." There was a pause, then, "No, we're not doing anything special tonight."

McKenzie prayed Sharon really meant that.

"No, don't come over here," Sharon said quickly. "Let's meet somewhere. We'll make plans when Mack calls you back."

Should she scream? Lilicat would hear her. But would she believe that McKenzie was in real danger and not just fooling around? And what would Sharon do?

"Okay, 'bye," said Sharon.

Silence. McKenzie listened intently. Blue, sitting on her chest, cocked his good ear, listening as well.

"You don't like her any more than I do, do you, Blue?" whispered McKenzie. "Smart cat."

Water running.

Sharon was taking a shower!

For the first time since she had awakened, McKenzie realized how long it had been since *she'd* been to the bathroom. Her face felt filthy. She had a horrible taste in her mouth. She must look horrible with her choppy bangs. And none of it mattered. None of it compared to what Sharon might do next.

Singing.

Sharon was singing in the shower! *"Oh my darling, oh my darling, oh my daaaarling Clementine!"*

At least she wouldn't be back for a while, Mack thought. In the meantime, she couldn't just lie here. She moved her head around as best she could, trying to take in the whole room.

Her first impression of the place had been accurate: It was a prison. Had she been sentenced to die here?

There had to be a way out.

So how come everything in her was saying there wasn't?

"You are lost and gone forever. . . ." Sharon's voice floated down the hallway.

"Dreadful sorry, Clementine."

There was really only one hope. She had to use her power to locate Brad. Maybe *he* could bring Sharon back to her senses. After all, when

Sharon saw that Brad was really alive, she'd forget all about revenge, right?

Eyes closed, Mack forced herself to focus on the image of the street outside Brad's dorm. She'd first felt his presence there once; if only she could feel it again.

In the background, she was vaguely aware of Sharon turning off the shower. She concentrated harder.

Then she saw it. A car.

It isn't black, and it isn't a Mercedes. It's red—a red Jeep. A young guy is driving. The car twists and turns down a country road. It whizzes past a road sign—Route 61. The car turns right. An on-ramp, I-97. Brad is driving.

Sharon was humming now. "I'll be with you in just a second, Mack," she called out cheerfully.

Block Sharon out. Concentrate!

Brad. Driving. More road signs flash by. He's headed north.

McKenzie could hear drawers opening and closing in a nearby room. Then footsteps coming closer.

Brad is off the highway now and on a dirt road. The road narrows, twisting and turning. The red Jeep bumps along through thick woods.

The key turned in the guest room door.

Another dirt road, and then he's there. A small, weather-beaten cottage, almost hidden by white trees. "Ten Birches," reads the small sign in the driveway.

"Mack? I'm back!"

Brad parks the Jeep out front.

"I told you I wouldn't be long."

The image faltered, disappeared.

McKenzie opened her eyes to see Sharon towering above her. In her arms she clutched Blue, who was yowling pitifully. Sharon pressed the shears into the skin of his throat.

chapter 16

"Don't! Stop! I found Brad," stammered McKenzie.

"Right. Where is he this time? In a Volvo?"

"No, a cottage."

Sharon waited.

"It's called Ten Birches, I guess because there are all these birch trees in front."

"If you're making this up . . ." Sharon threatened, but she pulled the shears back from Blue's throat.

"I'm not, I swear. Brad is alive, just like I told you. So I think it's time you calmed down and let me out of here."

Suddenly the shears were against Mack's

throat. "Not until I see that Brad is really alive. Where is this cottage?"

McKenzie tried desperately to think, to remember, to picture it all again. "Route 61," she gasped. "He started out on Route 61, going north."

"Yeah, and then?"

The road signs flashed past in McKenzie's mind. She tried to slow it all down, rewind the film somehow, freeze the images. "I-97, still going north."

"Good. Keep going."

"Exit 29. Bakersville."

"You're almost there."

McKenzie shut her eyes tighter. "Turning right at the . . . red horse."

"Red horse?"

"Flying red horse . . . a gas station . . . Mobil!"

"Don't stop, McKenzie," Sharon said urgently.

"Left onto . . . Briar Lane . . ."

"Good . . ."

"And right onto Kennicott." The narrow dirt road, the thick woods. There! Behind the white trees. "On the right. At the 'Ten Birches' sign."

McKenzie was sweating from the effort. She

opened her eyes. Sharon looked almost relaxed, almost normal.

"That's it," McKenzie said. "That's where he is. You've got to believe me."

Now it was Sharon's turn to close her eyes. "At last. At last," she murmured. She smiled. "I knew you could do it." She whirled around the room, did a pirouette.

McKenzie felt herself laughing. "He's alive," she cried hysterically. "I told you he was, I told you."

"Yes," Sharon said, moving out the door. "You told me."

"Sharon?"

Sharon turned to face Mack. "I'll be right back."

Then she was gone.

"I did what you asked me," Mack cried after her. "I told you exactly where he is. Now come back and untie me! Sharon!"

There was no response for a long while. Then the footsteps sounded again as Sharon returned. She stopped in the doorway, dressed in her green parka, zipping something into her purple shoulder bag. A gun.

"Where did you get that?" McKenzie asked.

"My mom got it after the divorce—since we

don't have a man around to protect us anymore.
I think it's going to come in very handy."

"What are you going to do with it?" Mack
asked desperately. "Where are you going?"

Sharon looked up. "I'm going to get Brad.
He won't get away from me this time."

"What?!"

Sharon pulled out her car keys and idly swung
them back and forth. "Thanks for all your help.
Bye-bye, McKenzie."

The key chain.

McKenzie had noticed it before—the troll, the
silver mirror. The mirror caught the sunlight
from the high window and sparkled it right into
McKenzie's eyes.

She stared, transfixed.

But she was no longer seeing the mirror . . .

*Brad and Sharon. They're standing together.
Where? Outside Brad's dorm.*

"You said forever," Sharon says, her voice loud.

*"I never said that," Brad says. "Never." His
hand slices the air.*

"Forever," insists Sharon. "It was our word."

*"It was your word, Sharon," corrects Brad. "I
never . . ."*

*But Sharon just keeps staring at him with those
large blue eyes, that hopeful smile. "Oh, but you
did, Brad. You said you wanted to marry me."*

Brad throws his hands up in the air. "Forget it, Sharon. It's over."

Suddenly Sharon grabs him. She clings to him, weeping. "Don't leave me, Brad. Please. I love you."

He is trying to pry her fingers from his coat.

"No!" she screams.

Other students are walking by. All staring. She is making an incredible scene.

Finally, Sharon walks away. But she runs back almost at once. "Take me back," she pleads.

Brad shakes his head helplessly.

"You lied to me," Sharon says, spitting out the words.

"Sharon, I never lied to you."

"That's another lie!" She pounds her fists against his chest. He catches her hands and holds them.

"Sharon, I'm sorry." He speaks slowly, trying hard to get through to her. "I'm very sorry. But you've got this whole thing blown way out of proportion."

"No!"

"Can't you understand? I just don't feel that way about you anymore. It wouldn't be right to keep going out together. I'd just be leading you on."

Her head is bowed. The words are finally sinking in. Her grip loosens. Now the sobs come, racking her body.

She lets go. Moves away. "Please," she begs again. "I don't know how I'll live without you."

"Sharon, you'll get over it," Brad says. "Believe me. You'll get over it."

She shakes her head. She mouths a word. Never.

Then she reaches into the pocket of her coat. She pulls out her key ring. The reflective mirror flashes brightly, catching the last of the sun.

She goes to her car. Except it's not her red Audi. It's a black Mercedes.

She starts the motor. The troll with the orange hair bobs up and down as it hangs from the ignition key.

Brad is talking with some friends. They're concerned. Is everything okay? He assures them it is. Then he starts to cross the street. He's headed for the Store 24.

He's about halfway across the street when something makes him look up.

The black Mercedes is hurtling through the dusk, straight at him.

A look of terror crosses his face.

Sharon is going to run him down.

chapter 17

Stunned, McKenzie opened her eyes. "It was you!"

But the room was empty. Sharon was gone.

"Oh, no!" McKenzie gasped. Brad was still alive, but he was in terrible danger. She had just told Sharon exactly where to find him.

"Sharon!" McKenzie screamed. There was no answer.

She swung her legs over the bed. She tried to move forward—and crashed to the floor. Luckily, she managed to turn, so that she fell on her shoulder and side.

She was staring at a dusty floor. Up! Somehow, she struggled to her feet.

She shuffled forward with the tiniest possible

steps and finally made it to the door. The locked door.

Now what?

Only the fingertips of her hands were free to move. She inched closer to the doorknob, held it. Tried to turn it.

It was moving! Sharon hadn't bothered to lock it! Even so, it took McKenzie almost a full minute to open the door. Then she made her way down the long hallway—which seemed even longer, since she was moving only an inch at a time.

What if Sharon hadn't left yet? What if she was waiting around the next corner?

McKenzie stopped cold, trying to hear above the sound of her own heavy breathing. Nothing.

Come on, she coaxed herself. Baby steps. You can do it.

At last she came to the head of the stairs. The steep spiral staircase curved dizzyingly below her, as if inviting her to fall.

Easy now.

Suddenly—out of nowhere—a blur of whiteness charged forward.

McKenzie ducked, almost pitching headlong down the stairs.

It was only Buttons.

The little dog pranced around on its hind legs, its mouth open in a grin that showed off its glistening pink tongue.

McKenzie moved back and sat down on the landing. She'd better play it safe, she decided, and began bumping her way downstairs on her backside.

Hurry! she ordered herself. Hurry!

She heard a familiar meowing from the kitchen and moved toward the sound.

Blue was perched on top of the refrigerator, safely out of Buttons's way. At the sight of McKenzie, he leaped down from the fridge and landed on the table—right next to the thick-bladed silver shears.

It took several tries before McKenzie managed to pick them up. The blades fell open slightly. But she couldn't move her fingertips enough to close them. She would never be able to close them hard enough to cut the ropes. Her heart was pounding. What was that noise? She listened. Nothing.

Hurry!

She moved to the counter, then leaned against the shears, wedging them between her and the top drawer. The sharp blades jutted upward. She positioned her bound hands over the blades and raked them backward. Forward. The shears shifted. She pressed harder with her hips, pressed with all her might.

She was sawing now, rubbing the ropes again and again. Once she slipped and the edge of the blades rubbed against her flesh. She gasped but kept going.

Finally, the rope began to fray. A few minutes later her left hand was free. She could grip the shears now. She positioned the blades around another one of the ropes that bound her.

McKenzie thought of Sharon holding the shears to Blue's belly. She tried to push the nightmare image out of her mind as she squeezed the blades shut with all her might.

In a few minutes, all the ropes had been cut. Mack rushed to the phone. "Officer Rizzuto, please," she whispered.

"Could you speak louder, please," someone answered gruffly.

"Officer Rizzuto."

"Officer Rizzuto isn't in," said the gruff voice.

"It's an emergency," McKenzie said. She backed against the wall, clutching the shears in one hand, half-expecting Sharon to leap out at her any moment.

"Do you want to report a crime?"

McKenzie didn't know what to say. "I want

to report a crime that hasn't happened yet. One that's going to happen."

"Uh-huh." The policeman waited.

"Look, when will Officer Rizzuto be back?"

"Probably not till tomorrow. But I can leave her a message."

"Tomorrow will be too late," McKenzie said breathlessly. "Send a police car right away to—" She rushed through the directions to the cottage. She wasn't sure the policeman was even listening.

What was she doing? Sharon was probably already on her way up north. Every second counted. "Did you get all that?" she demanded.

"You still haven't told me what the trouble is," the policeman said after a pause.

McKenzie looked around the room in a panic. There was a clipboard by the back door. On it hung a set of car keys. She pulled them off and stuffed them into her pocket. "I'll call back," she said, hanging up abruptly.

Then she reached down for Blue, who was rubbing against her legs. "We're out of here," she whispered.

Sharon's red Audi was no longer in the driveway. Were the keys in her hand a duplicate set? Or was there a second car?

McKenzie headed for the garage. The door swung up and open with a tremendous clatter.

The garage was dark, and the car inside was even darker.

The black Mercedes.

chapter 18

The speed limit on Route 61 outside of Lakeville was 55 mph. McKenzie was doing 70. How much of a head start did Sharon have? It didn't matter. She had to catch up!

But at the first rest stop she came to, Mc-Kenzie pulled off the road. She hurried into the bathroom. She couldn't remember needing to go to the bathroom this badly—ever!

When she came out of the stall, she rushed to the sink, washed her hands, and splashed some cold water on her face.

Then she looked in the mirror.

She almost screamed.

It was the face of a madwoman. Dark circles

under her gray-green eyes. Choppy bangs that looked as if they had been cut with a buzz saw.

McKenzie ran back to the Mercedes. Inside, Blue was curled up on the high back of the leather driver's seat, meowing silently through the glass.

Mack shifted the cat to the safety of the floor, then peeled out of the parking lot and back onto the highway, quickly passing the car in front of her. As she drove, she kept peering ahead for the red Audi whose license plate read FOR-EVER.

She passed another car, a green Toyota, but before she could pull back into her own lane, everything went black.

Sharon's face, filling her brain. The tiny smile. The blank blue eyes.

A shrieking car horn pulled McKenzie back to the present. She had moved back into the lane too soon, cutting off the Toyota behind her. She stepped on the gas, and the road ahead of her disappeared again. . . .

Brad gets out of the shower. Whistling. He's just come home from work. He reaches into the fridge for a soda, opens it. Sits down. Puts his feet up. Time to relax.

Again, McKenzie came out of it just in time. She was about to ride right up the bumper of the yellow Chevy in front of her. She hit the brake, just as she saw . . .

Sharon, slapping the steering wheel of her car. She has the gas pedal pressed to the floor. Her eyes are burning. She hunches over the wheel, urging the car forward like a jockey on a horse. Her blond hair blows in the stiff, cold breeze. A furious grimace distorts her face.

More horns blaring.

McKenzie pulled the car over to the side of the road. She clutched her head, moaning, as the images pounded through her brain.

Brad fixing himself a sandwich.

Sharon turning onto a dirt road that leads to his cottage.

Brad turning on the TV.

Sharon pulling up in front of his house, checking her purse to make sure the gun is there. Then checking to make sure the gun is loaded.

Brad going to answer the door.

Sharon standing there. Smiling.

Brad looks shocked, terrified. How did she find him there? Sharon takes the gun from her purse. She aims it at Brad.

"NOOOOO!" McKenzie screamed.

Her head suddenly clear, she immediately pulled back out into traffic, driving as fast as she could. I-97. Exit 29. Bakersville. Turn right at the Mobil station. Left onto Briar Lane. The dirt road. Narrowing. Thick woods. Another right onto Kennicott. The white trees. The little sign: TEN BIRCHES.

And there, parked out front, was the jeep. And the red Audi.

McKenzie raced for the cottage. Please let me be in time!

She tugged open the front door. "Sharon! Brad!"

Then she saw him.

Brad was lying facedown on the cottage floor, a dark puddle of blood slowly spreading across the shiny white linoleum.

McKenzie started to cry out, but she choked the sound back.

She was too late.

chapter 19

"Brad!"

McKenzie knelt beside him. His eyes were open, staring, unseeing. McKenzie was afraid she was going to faint. She turned away, ducking her head so that her blood would flow to her brain.

She had to get help. She stood up quickly. Too quickly. She felt herself begin to sway.

A hand reached out to steady her.

"Easy does it," said a soft voice.

McKenzie turned. Sharon was smiling at her. The gun was aimed right at her face.

McKenzie charged forward, knocking Sharon's hand up into the air. The gun fired and the bullet hit the ceiling.

McKenzie had both hands on Sharon's arm, the one with the gun. As Sharon tried to wrench her arm away, the gun fired again. There was the sound of shattering glass as the bullet blasted through the cottage's big bay window.

Summoning all her strength, McKenzie yanked Sharon toward the nearest wall and slammed her into it. The gun dropped from her hand. McKenzie dove for it, but Sharon kicked it out of the way. Then she kicked again.

That kick caught McKenzie in the ribs and sent her tumbling backward. Sharon raced for the gun.

But as she went by, McKenzie reached out a hand and grabbed one cowboy boot. Sharon went down hard.

Immediately, McKenzie was on her, bending an arm behind Sharon's back. "If you move, I'll break it," she threatened.

But Sharon's other hand reached back and flailed wildly, scratching McKenzie's cheek, poking her eye. Now Sharon was getting to her feet, lifting McKenzie with her. Sharon's face was clenched with fury and determination. Her hands were slapping at McKenzie, clawing her face, pulling on her hair.

McKenzie fell to the ground. She scrambled to her feet, ducked her head, and charged, punching and kicking with all her might. Both girls went down. Mack closed her eyes as they rolled over and over on the floor. Suddenly McKenzie rolled onto something heavy and un-yielding.

Then she opened her eyes.

She was staring straight into Brad's bloody face. His eyes flickered open. He moaned.

McKenzie screamed. But there was no one to hear her, she knew, out here in the woods. No one but Sharon and Brad, but he was helpless.

Sharon was now on her feet. Stepping quickly over Brad's body, she knelt down and snatched up the gun.

"It's too bad things had to work out this way," Sharon said, breathing hard, pointing the gun right at McKenzie. "We could have been such good friends."

chapter 20

"STOP! SHARON! WAIT!" McKenzie screamed.

The blank blue eyes seemed about to bore right through her. So did the dark barrel of the gun.

"My God! Are you really going to shoot me? Don't you know me? I'm McKenzie. McKenzie!"

Sharon's face was set hard. Her expression didn't waver. McKenzie rushed on, desperately trying to find a way past that blank face, into that closed heart.

"Sharon, you don't want to do this, do you? Think for a second!"

No response.

"And Brad—we've got to get him to the hospital—he's—"

The cold blue eyes. "I hate Brad."

"No, no—no, you don't hate Brad. You love Brad. You don't want to hurt him. Maybe we can still save him! Please, Sharon, listen to me!"

McKenzie tried to control her voice, but that was impossible. It was shaking wildly. "Sharon, you need help too. Lilicat and I can't do it for you. You need professional help."

Sharon's face was rock hard. "All I ever needed was help from my friends. But you never cared. You never even liked me."

"That's not true," McKenzie cried out. "Lilicat and I both like you. We liked you right from the start."

"No, you were just pretending to like me—just like Brad pretended to love me," said Sharon. She was smiling now, as if McKenzie were saying something terribly amusing. It was a crazy smile.

"No, Sharon, that isn't true."

Keep your eyes on hers, McKenzie ordered herself. Try not to glance down at the gun.

But that was impossible, too. Pointed right at her, the gun drew her eyes like a powerful magnet. Mack's whole body was beginning to shake, anticipating the deafening crack the gun would make when it went off.

"If you like me so much," Sharon said, still smiling, "how come you always sounded so annoyed when I called?"

"Sharon," McKenzie said desperately. "You've got to listen to me. I know what you need. You need love. More love than any one person can probably give you right now but—"

The gun moved. Sharon had raised it. Now it was pointed right at McKenzie's heart.

"You've got to let me help you. I'll stand by you while you get the help you need."

Sharon shook her head. "Brad deserted me."

"No," McKenzie surged on. "You scared him, Sharon. You pushed him away. You tried to run him over!"

"I know," Sharon said quietly, the smile finally fading.

"Sharon, please put that gun away. We've got to call an ambulance. Look at him! Please! Look!" McKenzie pointed down at Brad's body.

Sharon glanced down and quickly back up.

"Sharon, I don't know what happened to you to set you off like this, but I know it must have been intense. I know you've been through a lot. Your parents' divorce—"

Sharon twitched. McKenzie had hit a nerve.

"You must feel all alone, Sharon, like you don't mean anything to anyone—but you do. Don't lash out at the only people who can help you."

Sharon blinked. Her large blue eyes were starting to well up with tears.

"It's not too late, Sharon. You can reach out." McKenzie extended her hand toward Sharon. "I know there are people who can help you."

Sharon opened her mouth to speak, but no sound came out. It was as if there were no words for the pain she felt. A glistening tear ran down her pale cheek.

"I'm begging you, Sharon," McKenzie said, tears rolling down her own cheeks as well now. "I'm begging you to give me the gun. Give it to me, Sharon—please. . . ."

Sharon slowly lowered the gun.

"That's it, Sharon. You can do it. You can do it. Now give it to me. Give me the gun."

Sharon sniffled hard. She stared down at the gun in her hand. Then she took a step forward and dropped the gun at McKenzie's feet.

Sharon's face seemed to disintegrate before McKenzie's eyes. She was crying, horrible sobs that shook her whole body. McKenzie picked up the gun and pocketed it. Then she reached out slowly and put a trembling hand on Sharon's back. At her touch, Sharon fell forward, sobbing against McKenzie's coat. She suddenly seemed smaller.

"It's going to be okay," McKenzie said as soothingly as she could. "But we've got to get help."

She hurried to the phone and dialed the operator, asking to be connected to the police. As she blurted out directions to the cottage, Sharon kneeled at Brad's side.

McKenzie watched from the phone as the girl suddenly screamed, "He's still alive!" Sharon smiled crookedly through her tears.

"Please hurry!" McKenzie yelled into the phone. "Hurry!"

chapter 21

"Hold on a sec," the police officer told Mc-Kenzie. He typed quickly, grimly. "Okay. Go on."

Even as she looked around the bustling police station, Mack still couldn't quite believe that the nightmare was really over.

"After Sharon left his hospital room," she said more slowly, "Brad talked to me a little. He told me that he had been so terrorized by Sharon that he secretly left school, just to get away from her."

The officer, whose ID tag read LT. PEPITONE, clattered away on the keys. Then he said "Go on" again.

"Brad's been hiding out at his uncle's cottage

and working at his uncle's factory for the past few months. But now that Sharon is out of his way, he can go back to school—as soon as he's well enough."

"She's out of his way, all right," Lt. Pepitone said as he finished typing McKenzie's statement. "She's under arrest."

"She needs psychiatric care," Mack said.

"She'll get that, too, believe me." The policeman eyed her closely. "You sure *you're* okay?"

McKenzie suddenly realized that she had begun to tremble again. From behind her, a hissing radiator filled the small office with heat, but she was freezing. Still, she nodded vigorously. "Can I go now? I think my boyfriend . . ."

Lt. Pepitone scrolled the paper out of the machine. "He's right outside."

McKenzie found Aidan pacing outside the door.

When he saw her, his mouth dropped open. "Oh, no—" He rushed toward her, but she stepped back with an instinctive wariness that surprised both of them. He stared at her, his gray eyes filled with concern. Slowly, he reached out and touched her lopsided hair. "Wow."

"Don't say a word," she said.

Then she fell forward into his arms and let him give her a long, hard hug.

"Don't worry," he said. "I won't."

"Somehow I doubt that," she murmured into his sweater.

"All right," he said finally. "Don't take this wrong, but how long do you figure it will be before those bangs grow out?"

Mack made a face at him, but she couldn't hold it for long. She playfully punched his arm. "You!"

"Not that you don't look great in them," Aidan went on. "They're actually kind of funky. . . ."

An evil spirit claimed her best friend...

**THE
POWER #1**

The Possession

by Jesse Harris

McKenzie Gold's best friend, Lilicat, is thrilled
with the silk shawl she found at the flea market. It's
the perfect addition to her gypsy costume, and all
the guys seem to love her in it. But Mack doesn't
feel the same way. Lilicat doesn't act like herself
when she wears the shawl, and McKenzie just
knows that there's evil at work.

Mack's fears are soon confirmed: Lilicat is being
possessed by the ghost of the flamboyant Vanessa
Grant, who once owned the shawl. Scorned in
love, she's out for revenge—and her target is
Mack's adorable boyfriend, Aidan. Can McKenzie's
powers help her save Lilicat's soul, or will she lose
her best friend—and her boyfriend—to the venge-
ful spirit?

First time in print!

A Borzoi Sprinter published by Alfred A. Knopf, Inc.

It was a brutal murder, and she saw it all...

THE
POWER #2
The Witness
by Jesse Harris

It was a horrible nightmare...a young babysitter
viciously stabbed while the children slept. It would
have given anyone the creeps. But for McKenzie
Gold, it was even more terrifying, for her powers
told her that the murder had really happened, and
that she was the only witness.

Desperate to stop the murderer—and the violent
visions that haunt her—McKenzie goes to the
police. But they don't believe her story, and
McKenzie soon finds herself among the suspects.
It's up to McKenzie to find the killer—before she
becomes his next victim...

First time in print!

A Borzoi Sprinter published by Alfred A. Knopf, Inc.